THE LEGENDS OF REGIA

Verdant

a novella

TENAYA JAYNE

COLD FIRE PUBLISHING LLC

Other titles by Tenaya Jayne

Blue Aspen

The Slayer's Wife

Forbidden Forest

Forest Fire

ISBN: 978-0-9882757-5-1

Cover Art created by Erika Doucesse
Edited by Amanda Fiske & Jen Duffey
Proofread by Ally Robertson & Brynna Curry

COLD FIRE PUBLISHING, LLC
All Rights Reserved

PROLOGUE

Forest walked through the Onyx Castle's main entrance, a plain file clasped in her hands. She smiled at the security ogres and made her way down to the throne room. She peeked inside. Empty. It seemed like no one was ever in there. The thrones still stood in their usual places, but it was more of a museum now than a functional space.

Zeren was working hard to figure out how to transform the castle into a place that met the needs of the people. His efforts so far had gone largely unnoticed as the people, especially the vampires, had hardly wrapped their heads around the fact that they no longer had a king. But he pressed on, as did all of the new leaders.

Forest smiled to herself as she continued on her mission. She wasn't there to see Zeren, even though she'd have to find him and give him a hug before she went back to work, but she knew the castle was where she was most likely to find Redge. She really hoped the proposal in her hands was good enough to entice him to work for her full-time. If he hesitated or turned her down, she was willing to sweeten the deal in almost any way he wanted, and she wasn't above begging.

In the past months that Forest had come into her position as Hailemarris, Redge had proved, many times over, his usefulness to her as an investigator. She needed him to lead her growing forensics team.

"Hey, Merhl," she called as she spotted the young ogre at the end of the hall. "Is Redge here today?"

Merhl walked up to her and gave a little bow. "A pleasure to see you, lady, as always. Redge is out today. Would you care to see Zeren instead?"

Forest gave him a warm smile. "Do you know where he is?"

"In the memorial chamber, my lady."

Forest frowned. She knew Fortress castle like the back of her hand, but she never spent much time in the Onyx castle, save for the short stint she lived there, but that had been very short. If she had ever set foot in the memorial chamber, she didn't remember it.

"Forgive the imposition, Merhl, but would you escort me there? I've no idea where it is." She stood next to him and took ahold of his massive forearm.

Merhl smiled and blushed under his mottled copper skin. "No imposition."

He led her down a level and through a length of winding halls to an ancient and ornate door.

"Here we are. It is customary to whisper in the memorial chamber out of respect for the dead."

"Thanks for the heads up."

Merhl looked down at her hand still on his arm, focusing on her ring. "Is that...?"

"Yes. It's the End of the Bridge you made special for me. I had the idea of turning it into a ring. Dead useful. I use it all the time. I can't thank you enough."

"I'm happy to have been of service, my lady...and again I'm so sorry for—"

"No more of that, Merhl. It wasn't your fault," she said sternly.

He blushed again and looked at the floor. Forest wondered if he'd ever forgive himself for being victimized and tricked into releasing Leith.

"Thank you." He kissed her hand and walked off with slumped shoulders.

Forest made a mental note to tell her father to send Merhl more commissions. She pushed the heavy door open. Its hinges groaned forebodingly like a sound effect in a movie. *Theatrical indeed*, she thought as she stepped into the dark, torch-lit room. Stone walls stood in front of her and stretched sideways the length of the room. Names were carved into the stone. Touching sentiments like eulogies celebrated some. There were occasional carvings and likenesses of the deceased. The dancing firelight gave the carved faces a lifelike movement.

"Zeren?" She tried to keep her voice down.

"I'm back here," his voice came over the wall.

Forest moved to the end of the wall and found another row and then another before finding her father-in-law. Zeren was looking hard at a bare spot, thumping his finger against his lips. He looked up and beamed at her.

"Hey, there's my girl. I wasn't expecting to see you today... Oh dear, did I miss a meeting?"

Forest chuckled. "Don't worry. You didn't miss anything. I just stopped by to see Redge."

Zeren narrowed his eyes at her and glanced at the file in her hand. "What are you up to?"

"I was going to offer him a job."

Zeren groaned. "Not Redge! You've already taken too many of my staff. He'll never accept, just wait and see."

"Care to wager on it?"

He snorted. "No, thank you."

He held his arms out for her. Forest laid her cheek against his chest as he hugged her tight.

"I've never been in here. What are you contemplating so hard?"

"Oh, this is the memorial wall for all the past queens. I assume Christiana is still alive, wherever she is, but she may as well be dead...and being as *unpopular* as she was, well, I think if I don't put her up soon, I never will and I don't know who else would go to the trouble...and she was the queen after all. I don't figure on gushing, just something simple and to the point." He shrugged. "I feel obligated. It doesn't offend you, does it?"

Forest shook her head. "No. I wouldn't have Syrus if it weren't for her. I can honor her memory for that, if nothing else."

Zeren patted her shoulder. "Would you look at some of the other ones and give me an idea whose I might copy? In size and style, I mean."

"I can look for a few minutes, but I need to get back to work before long."

"Thanks." He turned back to the blank space and resumed thumping his finger against his lips.

Forest wandered down the wall, looking at the dead queens' memorials. It was easy to pick out the ones who were loved. And the ones who were hated.

The torchlight glinted off something shiny at the end, drawing Forest's attention. The memorial was carved in great detail. A twisted crown of branches with an inlaid iridescent stone in the center crowned the head of the woman. The similarity of the face to one she held dear, was striking. Then she read the inscription, her mind stumbling.

Queen Shi. My only and forever love. My true queen. No one could ever compare to you. When I die, may my soul find yours again. —King Leramiun

"What the fraz?" Forest mumbled, reading the inscription over again.

"Find anything interesting?" Zeren asked.

"That's an understatement."

"Huh?"

Forest pulled her smart phone out of her pocket and took a picture of the memorial. "I'm sorry, I've got to go. Something's come up."

Forest rushed out of the memorial chamber and turned her ring into her palm, so the End of the Bridge rested in her hand, thinking of the wolf's wood, as a portal opened for her. Forest landed flat on her feet in the wood, the portal closing behind her.

She waited, giving Shi a moment to notice her presence and read what was in her mind. Forest sighed when Shi didn't come out and address her.

"*Lucy, you've got some 'splaining to do,*" she called up through the branches of the trees in a decent impression of Desi Arnaz. "It's a helluva thing to find out you've been deceived for so many years, by someone you love...come on, Shi. Come out and talk to me. I'm not leaving until you do."

Forest walked a little. Shi remained quiet. "There's a real twist in the plot of the history you told me. Something major you left out. I've got a picture of a queen's memorial, inscribed by the hand of King Leramiun. Want to see it?"

Shi appeared right in front of her, an aghast look on her face. Forest pulled her phone out and held it up for Shi to see. Shi came closer, looking at it intently.

"Funny how you told me about the crimes of *the evil King Leramiun,* and how much you hate him, never once did you tell me you were mated to him. That's quite a juicy detail to leave out...I mean, what the hell, Shi!" Forest yelled. "You were the queen! How did you end up mated to the vampire king who killed your entire race? I thought you hated him!"

Shi's eyes moved from the small screen onto Forest's face. Her eyes widened as ghost tears pooled on her eyelids, and her bottom lip quivered.

"I...hate, yes," Shi said breathlessly. "But only because I loved him so much." Shi shook her head and cast her eyes to the ground. "I can't talk about it." She pressed her hand against her chest. "It hurts so much...even now. I'm sorry I didn't tell you the whole truth, but I felt if I never said the words aloud, I could convince myself reality wasn't real. The lie was for my benefit, not yours."

For a moment she looked closely at the picture again before gasping and turning away.

"You didn't know about the memorial, did you?" Forest asked.

Shi shook her head. "No...I didn't know."

"The carving is not that good of a likeness. I could tell it was you, but...well you saw the picture."

Shi turned back to face Forest. She held her twig-like arms up. "I didn't look quite as I do now when I was alive. The likeness is accurate."

Forest's mouth fell open. "What did you look like? Show me."

Shi shook her head. "Be content with the picture."

"No way! You've got to show me! You've got to tell me what really happened."

Shi walked away. Forest followed. "I don't think I can. I haven't the courage to say the words."

"I'm not leaving until I get the truth from you. You owe me that. Remember all those years when I was young, and I'd come here, and we'd do nothing but verbally bash vampires? Then for me to learn this."

"You mated your own vampire," Shi threw at her.

9

"Yeah, so? I didn't try to hide it from you. Was Leramiun your Destined Life Mate?"

"No." Shi stopped walking and looked up through the trees.

Forest crossed her arms and stared at her. Shi glanced down at her then averted her eyes.

"Quit stalling and spill it."

"I can't...I *can't*."

"I swear, Shi. You start talking or I'm going to sing."

A shudder swept over Shi. "Please don't! This wood has suffered too many crimes as it is without your caterwauling."

"Then talk."

Shi looked at her desperately.

"Suck it up, buttercup. Put your big girl panties on."

"All right, come with me," Shi said resigned.

She wrapped her branchy arms around Forest and swept her up and through the wood to the waterfalls. It wasn't the first time Shi had physically moved her from one side of the wood to the other in her uncanny, ghostly way, but Forest never liked the sensation. Shi dropped her on the sand and walked to the edge of the silvery violet water.

"Look," she said, leaning over the bank.

Forest stood beside her and glanced down. "My, my," she said quietly looking at Shi's reflection. "That's what you looked like when you were alive?"

"Yes."

"Well, it's no wonder you were the queen. Quite the Helen of Troy."

"What?" Shi asked.

Forest smiled at her. "You were gorgeous! I mean, you still are, but you didn't look like a walking tree back then."

Shi half smiled. "No. When I was in my corporeal form, I just looked like an ordinary woman."

Forest looked back at the reflection and snorted. "Yeah, real ordinary. You were breathtaking."

"That's what Ler used to think, too."

"Ler, huh? Okay, you've got to tell me now."

Shi groaned and walked off toward the Heart. Forest watched her from the side of her eye as she kept pace. Shi looked exhausted. She ghosted through the dense foliage of the ribcage while Forest struggled against the overgrowth. The pain of approaching the Heart began to pull in Forest's core.

"Why are we getting so close to the Heart?" Forest asked. "You know I can't stand to approach it."

"I'm taking you to where my memories live...I have to show you. I can't stand to tell you. I'm likely to stretch the truth. I can't tell you in an unbiased way. And this way, you can see Leramiun's memories as well."

The dancing flames of the manifestation dazzled Forest's eyes, as it always did. She was happy to see the flames were not as black as the last time she'd seen them. They were a smoky gray. The leaves of the crystal trees circling the flame chimed in the breeze, a melancholy tune, in line with the Heart's mood. Forest tried not to listen, but the notes sank deep inside her, bringing her mood parallel to the Heart's.

Forest hissed in pain and stopped walking. "I can't get any closer, Shi."

"Just wait here then."

Forest watched Shi move toward the flame with no idea what she was about to do. Shi stopped next to one of the crystal trees and laid her hand on its trunk before bending over and lifting a handful of shadow sand from around the tree's roots. She brought it back to Forest, the grains slipping quickly through her insubstantial fingers.

"Take it, before I lose it all."

Forest cupped her hands under Shi's and caught the sand.

"You want the truth, sniff that."

"What?!"

"Suck the sand up your nose."

"No freakin' way! You want me to trip out on shadow sand? Have you lost your mind?"

Shi shrugged. "Do it or don't. I don't care. It's the only way you'll get the story out of me."

"How?"

"This sand has sat, guarded in my roots, for centuries. It holds my memories."

Forest looked at her dubiously for a moment and then over to the crystal tree she took the sand from. "That's you?" she asked, pointing at the tree.

"Yes."

"I thought your tree was farther out. I thought it was the one I fell asleep against as a youth, when you first appeared to me."

"No, that was just where I was resting that day."

Forest looked back at the sand in her hand. "You said I could see Leramiun's memories, too. How is that possible?"

"Because..." Shi closed her eyes, pain clear on her face. "This is where he died."

"What? How did—"

"Stop asking me questions, Forest! Just take the sand."

Forest grimaced at the sand. "Man, I do not want to do this," she whined.

"Suck it up, *buttercup*," Shi said mockingly.

Forest shot her a dirty look, held a finger to one of her nostrils, and sucked the sand up her nose. For one second, nothing happened, and then she fell on her hands and knees, her head twisting in a knot. The ground shook under her, the surface sliding away, as Forest looked up into a very different wood than the one that had just been. Forest stood up, the Dryads moving around her. She backed up and watched history unfold before her eyes, knowledge of details of the time filling her head like a digital download. The rest manifested before her as though she watched a stage of players.

Chapter 1

The Dryads kept to themselves, aloof and arrogant. They were the chosen children of the Heart. Consecrated to protect and serve the wood and the flame that burned in the center. A race divided into three classes: breeders, warriors, and the Verdant. The Verdant, twenty princess trees circling the heart, existed to minister and commune with the flame, their roots pierced deep into the heart of the world. Protected from all the other races, the Verdant naïvely thought Dryads were alone in the world. The warriors held the perimeter of the wood, fighting off others in their corporeal form, never leaving a survivor to tell of what they encountered.

Those who died at the hands of the Dryad warriors were carried to a secluded spot and discarded. Bound to their trees, the warriors could only go so far. The bodies piled up over the years, forming a mass grave. The warriors hoped desperately that the grave was never found. And if it were found, it would invoke fear, not curiosity.

****

Shi held her breath, trapping the cry of pain in her throat, as her corporeal fingers dug into her own roots and broke off a section. Tears ran luminous down her cheeks, and sap bled from the self-inflicted wound. She stood up, carrying the root in both hands to the edge of the manifestation, and threw it into the white flames. The heartache and physical pain of losing part of herself quickly diminished as the flames ate her sacrifice, and the Heart imbued new life into the web of her roots, as a gift.

Shi bowed low and put both hands into the flame. Energy and life surged into her fingers as it had her roots.

"Thank you," she whispered before standing up and going over to the other Verdant, watching her perform her duties.

"Did you receive the blessing?" Mae asked.

"Yes."

"I wasn't sure you would when I saw the size of your sacrifice."

"Well, the Heart didn't complain, or withhold my blessing," Shi said defiantly. "Why do we have to sacrifice anyway? The flame burns regardless of what we do."

A few of the other Verdant gasped. Mae, the oldest, looked at them severely, and they all quickly walked away. When they were gone, she grabbed Shi roughly by the arm.

"You are the youngest Verdant, Shi, and instead of being silent and grateful, you ask incessant questions and stir up trouble. Why is that?"

"I'm sorry, Mae. I am grateful, it's just..."

"Just what?" Mae demanded.

"I'm just curious about things. Why are questions bad? I love the Heart. I just want to know why we do what we do."

Mae's face softened, and she let go of Shi's arm. "I sometimes forget you're little older than a sapling. I shall teach you the history after the next equinox."

"Why can't you teach me now?"

Anger flashed in Mae's eyes. "Stop your questions! I want you to stifle your curiosity until the equinox."

Shi looked at the ground. "Yes, ma'am."

"Now, you shall spend the rest of the day confined in your trunk."

"But..." she began then bit down on her lip at the look on Mae's face.

"Confined in your trunk until the moon rises, then you may come out and join the party."

"I wanted to go see Shea."

"You'll see your sister tonight."

"But, it's *her* party and everyone will be crowding around her, and I won't get a chance to talk to her."

Mae sighed and patted her shoulder. "It will have to wait, Shi. Use the time to contemplate your love for the Heart and how you might show it better the next time it's your turn to sacrifice."

Shi nodded, and Mae walked away, leaving her alone. She considered disobeying for a moment, but if Mae caught her, she would probably take her before the elders. Shi decided it wasn't worth the risk. She walked to her base and placed her hands on the bark for a minute before sliding into it. Alone, inside her trunk, Shi let her curiosity roam, asking herself questions she didn't have the answers to.

She resented Mae questioning her love for the Heart. Mae's derogatory tone about Shi's sacrifice in front of the other Verdant smarted, and a swell of spite began to grow inside her. It was still her day to sacrifice after all. She'd show Mae the meaning of sacrifice.

A plan began forming in Shi's mind, but once it was mature, she banished it. *Sacrifice must come from love to be accepted.* Her plan came back into her head as quickly as she'd dismissed it, only now it wasn't based on spite. She thought of the Heart, and the flame, and her vast love for them. And now that she'd thought of a sacrifice beyond any she'd ever given, it felt wrong somehow to offer less.

Shi poked her head out and listened. No one was near her. Chatter came from a distance. The afternoon would soon shift into evening, and the party would begin soon after. She didn't have much time. Climbing out of her trunk, Shi hesitated a moment, making sure there was no one around, before climbing up into her branches. White flowers budded next to her leaves. They were new, a part of the blessing she'd received earlier. Shi touched one of them gingerly before climbing higher.

She came to her favorite branch. The one for which she received the most compliments. Her breath was already coming in shallow gasps at the thought of what she was about to do. Why did love come with such pain? She grasped the branch in both hands, gritting her teeth, and quickly broke it off.

Every Dryad in the wood jumped and was frightened at the sound of Shi's cry of pain. Many ran toward the sound, sure of an emergency.

Shi's hands shook, and her tears burned as she held the branch to the flame. Pain screamed through her at the loss of the limb.

"I love you...I love you...I love you..." she said through sobs.

A cloud of dust flared up around the feet of the panicked crowd as they reached Shi.

"What have you done?" Mae demanded, pushing to the front.

"It's still my day, and I offered a sacrifice," Shi said, still prostrate on the ground in front of the flame.

"But you already--"

Mae's words cut off as everybody gasped together. The flame flared, reaching higher than anyone had ever seen it, white flames jumping onto Shi's hands and absorbing into her skin. Iridescent life surged through her whole body for all to see. Her hair and fingernails grew before their eyes and her skin shimmered.

The sound of bark cracking startled everyone again, and they all looked up at Shi's tree. The tree stretched up and out, growing bigger than any of the other Verdant. New braches filled her canopy, flowers budded and opened large and heavy in her leaves. Moss covered her bark in beautiful intricate patterns.

Shi stood up. Everyone looked on her with awe and fear. She didn't like it.

"I'm sorry to have disturbed you all. I meant for my sacrifice to be in private."

Everyone moved out of her way as she walked back to her tree and climbed inside. Murmuring began. Shi had established herself as the most devout Verdant to ever live, humbling everyone, including Mae.

Shi writhed inside her trunk. The Heart continued to pour life into her. It was too much. She was full and yet it continued to fill her. The surge made her giddy with pleasure, but ache and sting at the same time. Her branches continued to stretch upward, and she was powerless to stop them. Only when she began to cry did the surge subside. More than ever, Shi wanted to talk to her sister.

Shi waited for dusk before sticking her head out and looking around for the watchful eye of Mae. The way looked clear. She crept out quietly and ran to where Shea lived.

Most Dryads were breeders and experienced a greater level of freedom and community than the Verdant were allowed. As Shi entered their area, she noticed a marked difference in the way she was greeted. Friends and family she had known her whole life looked at her with apprehension and backed away. This new treatment shocked and upset Shi so much she feared she'd burst into tears before she got to her sister.

Shea sat on the ground, her back resting against the trunk of her mate, Hul, running her hand repeatedly over her pregnant belly. Shea smiled at Shi as she approached, a different kind of life shining from her. Shea noticed the troubled look in Shi's eyes. She patted the ground next to her.

"Oh, come here, little sister."

Shi sat down and nestled into Shea's comforting shoulder.

"What's the matter?"

Everything pent up inside her came rushing out. "Mae's always mad at me. Nothing I do is good enough for her. All the other Verdant seem happier than I do. They never ask questions. And I can't stop asking questions. I miss being able to be a part of everything. And you...You've got so much going on, you don't have time to watch over me anymore." Shi placed her hand on Shea's belly.

Shea stroked Shi's hair. "Growing up is hard. And it's true, I've got new responsibilities, but I'm still your big sister. You are always welcome to come and see me, and bother me with your constant flow of questions. Goodness knows I'm used to them."

Shi exhaled and relaxed against Shea. "Are you looking forward to your party?"

Shea chuckled. "Yes. I like getting presents. And everyone tells me you get the most with your first baby. But I think Hul is more excited about tonight than I am."

"If it's a girl, will you put her up to become a Verdant? She'll have the right root lines."

Shea pursed her lips. "No. I don't think so. I want my child to grow next to me and Hul."

Shi sighed. "That's good. You're already a good mother."

"Thank you. I want to be good."

They sat in silence for a few moments, a silence filled with the words they didn't need or want to say.

"So, I heard about your sacrifice, and I must say you've never looked more beautiful. I wish I could know what it's like to receive a blessing from the Heart. Is it wonderful?"

Shi shivered at the recent memory. "Yes. It's wonderful. But this time it was slightly painful as well. Overwhelming."

Shea lifted Shi's hand up to look at it more closely. "Wow. Look at your skin, Shi. I wish mine could shimmer like that."

"Your skin shimmers, Shea. Just differently, and more now that you're pregnant."

Shea smiled sweetly. "I guess it's just love." She groaned and arched her back a little. "Help me up, little sister. I've been sitting here too long."

Shi stood up and reached to grasp Shea's hand only to have Hul appear the next second and grab it before she could. Shi stepped back as Hul lifted Shea to her feet, wrapping his arms around her and kissing her mouth. And for a moment, Shea was lost in Hul, off in their own private world. It was always like that with them. Shi watched them for a second, voyeuristically. Fascinated and embarrassed at the same time.

Shea pulled back from him and blushed as her eyes met Shi's. "I'm sorry," she said quietly.

Shi looked away, seeing Shea thump Hul on the arm in her peripheral vision.

"I've told you to be more careful around Shi," Shea whispered to Hul. "She's not to know about such things. We've got to protect her innocence better."

"Sorry. You're right," he whispered back. "Shi!" he addressed her then in a loud voice. "Are you going to sit with us during the party?"

Shi met Hul's gaze then, feeling even more embarrassed. He was tall and strong, with a handsome open face. Shi had always liked him, and he made her sister goofy happy. But he was always overly passionate with Shea, and it made Shi feel strange at times.

"I'd love to sit with you, but the elders would never allow it. I need to stay with the Verdant."

"Oh, yes. Of course. That's proper. Well, we will miss having you with us."

The tears Shi had feared she would cry when she first came to see her sister started threatening again inexplicably. She held them back.

"Thank you. I must be getting back. The night draws on."

Shi hugged Shea quickly and fled before her tears escaped. She went back to her trunk and climbed inside, hating the emotion she couldn't deny was jealousy.

Chapter 2

Leramiun's crown threatened to slide off his head as he jogged down the hall, searching for Quinn. He was doing his best to fulfill all of his new duties since his father had died a month ago, leaving him the throne. For the life of him, Leramiun couldn't understand why Quinn seemed to be doing his best to trip him up. The sound of laughter and clanging metal directed him to the armory.

He pushed through the door. Irritation flared at the sight of Quinn and his friends, all stripped to the waist, sparring, and sweaty.

"Quinn! Did you forget the meeting? Again?!"

Quinn spun around, his smile turning into a sneer at the sight of his older brother.

"Well, look who it is," Quinn said sardonically. "Should we bow or curtsy? *Your Highness*."

The group of young men laughed. Leramiun cursed internally. He marched over to Quinn and sucker punched him in the face. Quinn crumpled at his feet.

"Get out!" Leramiun shouted to the group. They scattered.

Leramiun reached down and grabbed Quinn by the shoulders, hefting him to his feet.

Vitriol pooled in Quinn's eyes a moment before the tears. Leramiun pulled him into a tight hug.

"Dammit, Quinn. Don't challenge me in public."

"I'm sorry...I just...I miss Dad."

Leramiun blew out a heavy sigh. "I know. I do, too. But we've got things to do. We have to be men. You're Prince Regent now. I'm counting on you. I need your help. So, you've got to show me respect in front of other people. We can be ourselves, just brothers, in private. Okay?"

"Okay."

He gave Quinn a hearty slap on the back. "Clean up and get to the council chambers quickly."

Quinn nodded. Leramiun left the room, but as soon as the door closed behind him, a terrible crashing sound halted him in his steps. He stood still and listened as Quinn shouted and threw things around the armory. The sunken feeling in Leramiun's stomach dropped out even further as he listened to his brother's fit. He sighed and walked away. Experience had taught him not to try to console Quinn, it just made things worse.

Quinn had always been volatile, but since their father had died, he seemed to let his darker emotions run unchecked. Leramiun knew he needed to give Quinn more positive reinforcement, but he was just so damn busy he didn't have any leftover time or brain cells to figure out how.

Leramiun hurried back to the meeting waiting to start. He smoothed his shirtfront and made sure his crown was on straight before facing his advisors. All eyes turned on him as he entered the council chambers. He did his best to make his grimace into a smile.

Leramiun did all that he could to play his part. He talked, signed things, and broke up disputes among the table of old men, but his heart was hurting over his younger brother. Quinn took his sweet time showing up and was so flamboyantly disruptive when he came in and took his place, the elders looked pointedly at Leramiun to chastise him. He couldn't do it, not again after striking him in front of his friends. But, damn it, Quinn was begging for it.

Leramiun tried to appear interested in the scroll in front of him and thoroughly indifferent to Quinn's bad behavior. His head began to ache under the crown. Being king sucked. Whatever he did, people thought him to be either a tyrant or a weakling.

His eyes drifting over the words on the scroll slowed and began to take in the meaning until all of his focus was concentrated on the report. The talking in the room buzzed in his ears. He needed answers.

"Ho!" Leramiun held up his hand. Everyone quieted.

"Tell me about this," he ordered, tossing the scroll so it unrolled along the table.

Everyone leaned in to see, except Quinn who lounged back in his chair, picking at a thread on his cuff.

"What has been done about this?" Leramiun demanded.

"Nothing as of yet, Your Majesty. Since your father's death, everyone has been focused on your transition to the throne and securing it, ... A task we all admonish you to take more seriously. Your main goal right now should be choosing a queen with a powerful family to help build your foundation of friends."

Leramiun schooled his eyes mid-roll. "I told you I would choose my bride soon, and I will. But this..." He waved at the scroll. "Needs immediate attention. How long ago was it discovered?"

"Last week, Your Majesty. A courier stumbled across it. Gave him quite a shock, I can tell you."

All the old men chuckled.

Leramiun pulled the scroll back and looked at it again. *Mass grave found in the wilds south of The Lair.* The words seemed to jab a feather in his brain, tickling and annoying.

"I want this looked into now."

"It will take some time to form a task force, sire. Don't worry about it. Rest assured we are taking it seriously and shall report to you of our findings once we have any."

Leramiun clenched his fists. They weren't listening to him. His advisors didn't take his orders seriously.

"What else is there to discuss?" Leramiun asked the room in general.

Scrolls were read, a few little disagreements broke out, and Leramiun pretended to listen. A nagging pull began twisting inside him. His gut told him he was fast approaching something...the mass grave bothered him. He knew he must do something about it. Not someone else. It was important, Leramiun could feel it, he just didn't know how. He intended to find out.

The feather teased and tickled all day. He couldn't get his mind off the mass grave. The report didn't give details about how large it was. How old the bodies were, nothing. He got an idea in his head that he easily recognized as foolhardy, but that made it all the more seductive.

Before his father died, he'd been free to adventure, now he was trapped under the blasted crown.

Bad idea, he thought. *I'm going for it.*

After dinner, Leramiun made a point of making some off-color comments about his intention of visiting the harem before going to sleep. And he made sure he was seen escorting Helena back to his chambers. She was the most beautiful vampire in the harem, and he often enjoyed her, but she was a perfect alibi for what he planned and for possible future secret adventures he might take.

She smiled seductively up at him and sat down on the edge of the four-poster bed. Her smile turned to a look of shock as he roughly grabbed both of her hands and went down on his knees before her.

"Helena, I apologize if I have ever hurt you, or been unkind."

"My lord?"

"I need your loyalty now, not your body."

"Have I displeased you?" she asked sadly. "You no longer desire me?"

Leramiun took a deep breath. He didn't have time to soothe her feelings, but leaving her hurt and confused was a mistake he could not afford. Smiling, he kissed her hand.

"You are my favorite. You've always been my favorite. Don't ever doubt that, Helena. I have a special place for you in my heart, though it must always be secret."

Her pretty bottom lip came out in a perfect pout. "Because you have to choose a bride."

"Yes, yes. How I wish I didn't have to." He reached up and caressed her cheek. "If only I could choose you instead, what a queen you would be. But they would never allow me. I am caged."

Easy, harmless lies.

She simpered at him. "Poor thing. I'll always be here to comfort you. And you can favor me with a place of esteem in the castle."

Leramiun hid his smile. *Mercenary*, he thought. He got up and went to his dressing table, quickly selecting a gaudy ring with a blue stone, and brought it back to her. "Here," he laid it in her palm. "You shall have the finest clothes, and I pledge to you I shall never be with another from the harem. You shall be known as my chosen mistress."

Her cheeks flushed with pleasure and excitement. But he had yet to seal the deal.

"And," he continued. "You shall be moved to your own apartments in the castle. A special place just for you where we can be together...and you shall have a servant."

Huge tears rolled down her cheeks. "Oh, my lord, you've made me so happy!"

"Good, because I need you now."

She made to remove her dress. Leramiun stopped her hands.

"No. I wish I had the time, but right now, the way I need you is to keep my confidence."

"I don't understand."

"I am leaving. No one knows. I'm going alone. I will be back in three days, or less. Until I return, you shall stay right here in this room. Don't open the door for anyone. Tell anyone who asks that I am sleeping, or engaged with you, and I don't wish to be disturbed. Understand?"

She nodded.

"Good." He kissed her hand again. "When I return I'll make good on all I have promised you, unless you betray my confidence."

She clasped the blue ring to her heart. "I shall never betray you!"

Leramiun went to his closet and stripped out of his dinner clothes and into a plain shirt, trousers, and traveling cloak. He strapped on the plainest sword he could find in his room and slid a dagger into his boot.

"Do you think anyone will recognize me?" he asked Helena.

"Probably not, my lord. You have not been out of the castle much since taking the throne, have you?"

"No. In fact, I haven't been off the grounds since my coronation."

"You're not putting yourself in danger, are you?"

He shook his head as he reached into his top drawer and pulled out two silver balls hanging from chains. He hung one around his neck and smashed the other between his palms. Helena grabbed ahold of one of the bedposts for support as a portal opened and pulled at its surroundings. Leramiun winked at her before stepping into the rushing center of the portal. It closed after him, leaving Helena alone and windblown.

Leramiun stumbled as he landed on the uneven terrain. The shadow of the Lair stretched across the ground and injected cold into the night. He was just where he wanted to be; in between werewolf territory, the wild forests, and the ragtag camps of the shifters. The mass grave was supposed to be close by.

He pulled his hood up over his head and moved off into the thick trees away from the Lair. He listened carefully to the night around him. There was nothing. He began berating himself. *What the hell am I doing? Out here all alone with no guard?* And what could he learn in the middle of the night anyway? A mass grave could mean a number of bad things; new phantom guardians, confused and bloodthirsty, among other undesirable things. He wasn't an investigator. Why was he here?

Leramiun took a deep breath. This was where he needed to be, his gut persisted. He should just go home, choose a bride off that exasperating list, and behave like a king. He lifted the End of the Bridge hanging around his neck and held it in his palm. His fingers came down around it, pressing, when suddenly a noise startled him. Leramiun held totally still, not even daring to breathe when the sound came again...laughter...and music. He followed the sound deep into the darkness where the branches overhead shut out the moonlight.

CHAPTER 3

Shi smiled vaguely at anyone who caught her eye or spoke to her, wishing she could escape the party entirely. Being jealous of her sister was crude. But try as she might, the jealousy wouldn't go away. She was a Verdant after all, while Shea was merely a breeder. Shi held the place of reverence, so why couldn't she just join in the merriment with everyone else and be happy?

Why did she care? She didn't want a child. Did she? Shi shook the longing away. The Verdant were barren. Forbidden to love anyone but the flame. Shi placed her hand on her stomach and was overwhelmed with a moment of sorrow. She didn't even have a womb. How was it right that the grafter removed it in her infancy? No one asked her what she wanted.

Shea laughed and hugged a well-wisher who presented her with a gift. The joyful noise sounded in Shi's ears like a scream. She had to get away. Take hold of her base emotions so she, too, could wish her sister well and mean it, before the night was out.

She wove her way through the crowd to the outskirts. When she reached the boundary, no one seemed to be on guard, everyone was enjoying the party. She looked out at the dark, twisting arms of the wild and shuddered with an unusual desire to dive into it.

"Shi?"

She started at the sound of her name and turned around.

"Oh, Ree. You scared me."

The warrior gave her a little bow. "I'm sorry. What are you doing out here?"

"I just needed a little solitude."

He nodded. "You're a bit far out. I can't let you go any farther."

She smiled at him. "Don't worry. I wasn't going anywhere. I just wanted to see the stars."

He looked up. "Not a great night for them. Too many clouds. Well, you should head back. I'm the only one on guard right now. Nar is late. It's his turn to hold the boundary and let me go enjoy the party."

"Would you like me to get a drink and bring it to you?"

Ree blinked at her for a second. "Really? That would be great! Thanks, Shi."

"No problem." She turned and walked back the same way she'd come.

"I'll be in the east corridor," Ree called.

"Okay."

She walked a few more paces and stopped, listening. Ree walked off toward the east. Creeping as quietly as she could, Shi slid through the shadows and past the boundary. The rush of doing something new and off-limits spread through her. She'd never been out this far.

Shi ran her hands on the bark of the trees in the wild. None of them were like her. They were all bound, silent ones. They held their spirits deep inside and didn't walk in any corporeal form. Shi didn't know if she felt sorry for them or not. Maybe they were happy as they were.

As Shi continued farther and farther away from her home, a small pull in her back began to alert her she was going too far away from her other half. She wondered when she reached her limit would she break in two, or would she just not be able to move any farther? This might be her only chance to test it.

****

Leramiun walked cautiously through the shadows when he turned a bend and stumbled upon a crossroad, not a crossroad on a path, but one in the direction of his life. The previous road abandoned, the previous goal forgotten. He was unflinchingly convinced destiny had brought him here to this spot at this moment. All thoughts of thrones, brides, and politics simply vanished from his mind. Even his own identity was lost the moment he laid eyes on her.

Leramiun's pupils contracted against the luminescence of her skin. The glow radiating through her pores was blue-ish green, tinged with gold. The very essence of life shone from her. The pain of desire bit down deep as though a long sword impaled Leramiun's core. Was he dreaming? May he never wake. How could such a woman really exist? What race in Regia could produce such a goddess?

 He hesitated only a moment then his stride ate up the ground he could no longer feel under his feet. He was possessed and intoxicated. She was the cause and simultaneously the cure of this new pain inside him. She was the end of all, every goal, every battle, and every journey now ended with her.

His stride turned into a sprint, terrified she might vanish or run away.

****

Shi held still, spellbound, as she watched the stranger run toward her. A rush like a gust of wind rose inside her. Never had she seen anyone like him. The moonlight shone in his flaxen hair and glinted in his sky-colored eyes. His was the most beautiful masculine face she'd ever seen, and she instantly felt like a small child who cried *Mine!* at the sight of something desirable. The bud of her spirit lifted and opened like a rose. She saw herself in his beautiful strange eyes, and a pull seemed to bind around her as though he cast nets and ropes on her with only his eyes.

Then came the fear. What was about to happen? An innate instinct to flee, as prey does, overwhelmed her. But if she fled, it was because she desired to be captured. She didn't know what he was having never set eyes on any but her own kind. Why had she left the shelter and safety she'd always known?

Shi continued to hold still, torn between fear, fascination, and this new unknown desire to touch, to claim. Then it was too late.

He skidded to a halt three feet in front of her. What was he? How was she to behave? Shi surveyed him from his feet back to his strange blue eyes. His eyes let her in, let her see. He was falling inside himself, somehow dying and being reborn. She reached out and laid her hand on his chest, testing to see if he was like her, two beings at once. But as soon as she touched, she knew this was all of him: body and spirit together, unable to split apart.

A strange pain mixed with joy came into his face at her touch, and he laid his hand over the top of hers. The touch of his hand brought the flutter under her skin, at first like gentle wings. Then the wings grew heavy and beat the hell out of her.

"What are you?" Shi asked, retracting her hand.

He grabbed at it and went down on his knees. "From this moment, until the day I die...I am your slave."

He pressed his lips against her hand, sending a new storm of flutters under her skin. None of her kind would dare touch her in such a way.

Shi pulled her hand away and took a step back. "I have to go," she gasped.

He jumped to his feet, panic in his eyes. "Wait! Please, Lady. "

"What do you want?" She continued to back away.

"Do you not know? Is it not plain in my eyes?"

Shi looked back into the blue of his eyes, caught in their depths, and struggled to free herself from them. It *was* plain. He wanted everything: her heart, body, and soul. He wanted things she couldn't name and things she didn't understand. Shi's breath caught in her throat, and her cheeks flushed. "I have to go."

"Then I'll go with you."

"You can't! I've never seen one such as you before. I don't think you're allowed."

A small smile lifted his mouth. "There is nowhere in this world *I* am not allowed, Lady."

"What are you?" she asked again.

"I am a vampire. What are *you*?"

"A Dryad... One of the Verdant."

"What does that mean?" he asked. "Verdant?"

"I am one of the chosen, a princess, to keep and love the flame."

"Princess, huh? I like that."

"I have to go," she repeated.

"Please, tell me your name."

She hesitated. If she gave him her name, he would give his in return. If she knew his name, she would never be able to convince herself he was nothing but a dream.

"Please," he repeated.

"Shi...what's yours?"

"Leramiun."

Shi snorted. "Who has a name like that? It's so long! I'll call you Ler."

"Please don't leave...or if you must, promise to come back. I have to see you again, Shi."

"No! I've seen your eyes. You want things I cannot give. I serve the Heart. I sacrifice."

"I have to see you," he declared again adamantly. "I'll meet you here tomorrow night. I'll wait. I'll be here tomorrow and the next night and the next night and the--"

"Stop it! Go away! Forget me."

"You request the impossible, Shi."

"So do you!"

"I could never forget you. Never would I want to. Do you think you could forget me?"

A terrible shaking began inside her core. "I want to forget you," she whispered.

She walked away from him. Silence and darkness enveloped her. She walked a few more paces before turning around. He was gone. Shi listened. There was no sound. At first she felt relief, then those terrible wings filled her up again, only now they fluttered with knife edges, cutting her up. Her beautiful dream had vanished.

Suddenly he stepped out from the shadows in front of her and took her in his arms.

"Forget this!" he said, pressing his lips against hers.

Her whole life seemed to shatter around her. Everything she knew her life was and would always be had stretched uninterrupted before her, and now, one bizarre moment had torn that knowledge to shreds. Shi trembled against him, a tear escaping her eyes as he stole a piece of her innocence and replaced it with a knowledge and a hunger that was as painfully sweet as it was taboo.

He released her slowly.

"I'll be here tomorrow night. If you don't come, I'll accept you were able to forget me after all. And I'll never come back again."

Shi wrapped her arms around herself, trembling.

"You had no right!"

He reached for her again. She shrank back.

"You don't know what you have done!" she cried.

Before he could say anything else, she ran, disappearing into the darkness.

CHAPTER 4

Shi curled up inside her trunk, gazing restlessly at the moon hanging over her branches. The party had ended and everyone around her was quietly sleeping. She ran her fingertips over her lips. The shivers ebbed and flowed through her core as she contemplated what had happened to her. She had been defiled. Would the Heart still accept her sacrifices? Would everyone notice a change in her?

As the moon began to set, Shi's worry shifted into anger. She didn't do anything wrong. It wasn't her fault. It shouldn't change anything about her status as a Verdant. No one need ever know. It wasn't her fault, she thought again. Or was it? She broke the rules and ventured past the boundary alone. Boundaries there for her protection and look what had happened.

An unconscious smile broke over her face, surprising her. Yes, look at what happened. The shivers came back like soft pinpricks as she remembered every detail of her encounter with the vampire. She wouldn't forget him, not ever. He said he would wait. So what? Did that mean she would see him again? Curiosity, anticipation, and shame spread through her as Shi discovered a new capacity she'd never even contemplated she could harbor.

Shi hadn't slept at all by the time the sun broke the horizon, but she still felt energetic and oddly light. She had a secret. She'd never had a secret before, and it both terrified and excited her. Her normal level of curiosity surged into a new monster with new questions she couldn't ask anyone. The desire to talk to her sister, Shea, and tell her the secret and ask her what it was like to be touched by another person overwhelmed Shi. Could she ask in such a way that Shea would just think it was Shi's idle curiosity at work?

Shi thought of Ler again before leaving the confinement of her trunk. His eyes, his voice...his lips, and again she shivered.

As soon as her feet touched the ground, Shi froze in fear. All the other Verdant stood waiting for her. Nineteen pairs of eyes held her in place. They must have felt her defilement. They were going to remove her from their circle, or banish her to the wilds, or kill her. Pleas and excuses began rushing up her throat.

Mae stepped forward and stooped into a little bow to Shi. All the others followed suit. Mae straightened and placed her hand on Shi's shoulder.

"We, the Verdant, praise you, Shi. For showing us what real love and sacrifice is, we place you in a position of honor and authority. Will you accept this position and be our example?"

Shi's mouth fell open. "Yes," she squeaked.

****

Leramiun paced his bed chambers, his mind caught in a web of fantasy. Helena slept in his bed, undisturbed by the morning light or the shuffling of his feet. He didn't see her. His eyes were open, yet they perceived nothing in his surroundings. All he could see was Shi.

The earliness of the day mocked him ruthlessly. There were so many hours until he could go back to see her...if she came back at all. How would he go on if she didn't? What would he do if she did? If he never saw her again, at least he'd stolen a kiss...at least he had that. Then guilt slammed into him as he remembered the way she trembled and ran from him. Yes, stolen indeed.

"Oh, you're back...Majesty? Your Majesty? *Hello*?"

Helena's voice scratched in his ears like gravel. The vision of Shi disappeared. Helena sat in the center of the bed, disheveled by sleep. How had he ever thought her beautiful? How could he ever be with anyone except Shi now? The very thought made his flesh crawl.

"Did you find anything last night?"

Just my soul.

"Yes, but I need more time to look into it. I need you to continue to cover for me when I leave again."

"Of course, sire."

Helena looked at him expectantly for a moment. When he said nothing, she shrugged, laid back down, and covered her head with the blanket.

Leramiun contemplated what he needed to do next. Sighing deeply, he took off his plain clothes and dressed normally. He picked up his crown and held it in both hands. For something that was so exquisitely constructed and designed to be light, the responsibility it carried was so heavy.

He had daylight to kill. It was time for school.

The royal library was empty except for the librarian who scowled at him from his perch in the corner when he entered, as though Leramiun were a wayward child and not the king.

"What do you want," the librarian said in a voice as dusty as the back shelves. "Sire?" he added belatedly.

"I need information about Regia's forests and those who dwell there."

"What do you mean? The phantom guardians?"

"No. I mean the Dryads."

The wrinkles on the librarian's forehead layered up as he raised his eyebrows. "Dryads? I don't know that name, sire."

"You can't be serious."

"I assure you I am. I have never heard that word before. Where did you learn it?"

Leramiun hesitated a moment before taking a step back. "Never mind." He fled from the library, colliding into Quinn in the hall.

"Watch it, jerk!" Quinn snapped.

"Sorry," Leramiun mumbled, his mind elsewhere. He glanced at his brother, barely registering the veiled wrath behind his eyes. When he looked again, it was gone. He couldn't deal with Quinn right now.

He went back to his room. Helena didn't even stir as he entered. His mind was racing. How could it be? Had he really discovered a Regian race that no one (or at least no one he knew) knew about?

He considered all the angles he could think of in this situation. He was the King of Regia. These people were his subjects, even if they didn't know it. They might want to be a law unto themselves, but he wouldn't allow that. He assumed the Dryads must be connected somehow to the mass grave. If he found that to be true, steps would have to be taken. Leramiun considered the means of diplomacy he might use.

A smile curved his mouth. If Shi didn't come back to see him tonight, she'd see him again anyway as he forced his way into her world and discovered its secrets, as was his right and duty as the king. She could try to hide, but he would plague her, wearing at her resistance until she surrendered and gave him her heart.

Leramiun looked out his window at the day and counted the hours before nightfall. His heart picked up its pace. She *would* come to him tonight.

And if she did, all these other issues could wait. He'd put the world on hold, without hesitation, for Shi.

As the day dragged slowly on, Leramiun's mind flitted briefly over his responsibilities. If there was something he was supposed to do that day, and there always was something, he ignored it completely. He paced, looking at the same lines in the stone floor over and over until he couldn't stand being idle any longer.

He looked around his room, coming back to a level of normal lucidity in the afternoon. Helena sat in the far corner reading a book. He looked out the window and felt a rush of urgency. The afternoon was lengthening. He needed to get ready. He bathed meticulously and took his time choosing his clothes. At first he laid out his finest, wanting to impress Shi, but then on reflection, decided he wanted to look more relaxed and accessible. He had moments when his nerves overtook him, and he had to breathe deeply and refocus. Shi made him feel like an inexperienced, lovesick schoolboy and not a king, used to taking what he wanted when he wanted it.

Finally, after rubbing a little scented oil, designed to attract, on his skin, he dressed in soft black fabrics and put on the cloak he'd worn the previous night.

"Leaving again?" Helena asked as he rummaged through his drawer, grabbing two more portals and pocketing them.

"Yes. Don't wait up for me."

Helena seemed to scrutinize him then, one eyebrow raised and a small frown on her lips. He looked down at himself, self-consciously.

"What? Why are you looking at me like that? Does something look wrong?"

She opened her mouth then shut it again, shaking her head. "No. Nothing about you looks wrong."

"All right." He sighed. "I'll see you later."

He smashed the End of the Bridge and left.

He landed in exactly the same place as he had last night. Leramiun took in his surroundings more carefully in the evening light. The faint smell of smoke and dinner cooking drifted under his nose from the direction of the shifter camps. The werewolves' mountain stood like a jagged shadow in the distance, all black, with the tapestry of sunset behind it.

Leramiun took a deep breath and walked toward the place he'd laid eyes on Shi, making a mental map of the area as he went. Then he saw it. Above the branches crossing over his head, a line of trees jutted out, three times taller than the rest of the forest. Leramiun gaped. They were living monuments, visibly imbued with life, making every other tree he'd ever seen look sickly pathetic.

He approached them with a sense of awe, but the closer he came...a strong instinct surged into his gut, and he stopped. He sensed a warning. Danger. Instinctively, Leramiun knew this must be where Shi and her kind lived. He came no closer but moved off to the side to see what else he might discover about this protected vault of virgin forest.

****

The forest went to sleep around Shi. She kept still. She grasped the night in her hands, trying to keep it motionless, but it slowly slid through her fingers like water. He was out there...waiting for her. She wanted to go, but she was too afraid to move. Fear ran all though her. Not the fear of being caught. The fear of what churned inside her.

No, she would stay still and not see Ler again. The night would slip away, and the morning light would save her. Her life would stay the same. It was better to never know. Better to never taste. Shi ran her finger over her lips, caressing the memory of his kiss. She had already tasted. She closed her eyes, a single tear running down her cheek as her foot touched the ground. She looked up at the moon and let the night take her.

****

She'll come. She has to come.

Every rustling leaf and whisper of wind had him jumping, looking around for her. But there was only darkness. Would she be able to find him? Should he search for her?

She'll come. She has to come, he thought again for the hundredth time.

He wouldn't give up. He'd wait all night, till the morning chased away every trace of darkness. He'd stay right here and wait for her. But with every passing moment, he lost hope by small degrees, his heart turning brittle, threatening to break like dry clay.

From the corner of his eye, out of the blackness, came a shimmer of moonlight. His heart faltered. She made no sound as she walked, the breath of a gown she wore seemed spun from the stars. He thought he would die of happiness. She came! Of her own will, she came to him!

Fear radiated off her skin, but she kept walking toward him.

"Hello...Ler," she whispered, blushing.

"Hello, Shi."

She met his gaze for a second then looked down at her feet.

"So, you couldn't forget me after all?"

She shrugged her perfect shoulders and shook her head in a type of defeated surrender. "How does one forget being assaulted by a stranger? A stranger who clearly doesn't know that a Verdant can never be kissed."

"You're right. I'm sorry. I didn't know."

Her iridescent eyes cut right through him. "Had you known, would it have stopped you?"

"Well, I..." He sighed and smiled. "No. I suppose not. But I would have done it differently had I known the depth of your innocence."

A quick flash of interest sparked in her eyes. "Done it differently? How?"

"Shall I demonstrate?"

Shi gazed at his lips for a second before fear widened her eyes, and she took a step back. "No."

They looked at each other, staring, dissecting, and simply enjoying the view. The voluminous silence in the space between them transmitted meanings, thoughts, and desires, but to Shi, it was all in a foreign language. She didn't really understand, but the nuance of the silence frightened her. It seemed dangerous.

"Why did you come back?" he asked.

"I had to. I was curious...I'm sorry. It's shameful."

"What's shameful?"

"My curiosity. It's my worst flaw. I think the grafter would have tried to remove it from my roots when I was a baby, had he known."

The smile on her face led him to believe she was making some kind of joke. It didn't sound funny to him.

"What are you talking about?"

"Nothing. Never mind."

The words *grafter* and *roots* caught in his mind. "I tried to learn some things about you today, but my library proved worthless."

"What is a library?"

He looked at her incredulously for a moment, then he realized she was serious. Without thinking, he stepped toward her and touched her cheek gently, mesmerized by the shimmer under her skin.

"What are you?" he whispered. "I don't understand..."

Shi swallowed hard and placed her hand on his chest as she had the night before, feeling the beating of his heart.

"This is all of you," she said slowly. "Your body, spirit, and mind all go together. You cannot separate the pieces of you. It is not so with me. I have two...parts. What you see and touch, my corporeal form, thinks and feels as you do, but I am tethered to my other, silent half..." She hesitated, unsure of the outcome of proclaiming the truth. "A tree."

He frowned. After a moment, he looked down at her hand on his chest and placed his hand over hers.

"Strange," he said quietly. "You don't mean you're somehow bound to this forest, but one actual tree?"

"Yes."

His gaze hooked deep into hers and held her immobile. Then he smiled, bemusedly.

"It changes nothing, Shi. I still feel the same way."

"You do?"

"Yeah. I do. But how do you feel? Do you know any more about my race than I know of yours?"

Shi giggled. "I only needed to touch you to know that this is all of you. Aside from that, I don't know anything about vampires. You're the first one I've ever met."

Then it was his turn to be nervous as he described his need for blood.

"That is an...odd weakness," she said.

He shrugged. "I guess you're right. I've never thought about it before now. We are very different."

"Different, yes, but we seem to be similar in at least one way."

"Oh? What's that?"

"Well, we're attracted to each other," she said plainly.

Her declaration made his heart leap. She noticed the change in his pulse, her hand still against his chest.

"Are you all right?"

He threw his head back and laughed. "Yes, Shi. I don't know if I could be any better at this moment."

She frowned. "You are certainly strange."

He laughed harder. "I love how you just say things. You're not trying to be coy or manipulative."

"I don't understand."

He stopped laughing abruptly. She looked upset and pulled her hand out from under his and took a step back.

"I'm sorry. I wasn't mocking you. I've just never met anyone like you."

"I thought we'd established that."

"I mean your personality... You're so pure and honest."

"Of course I am! I'm a Verdant."

"What does that mean, Shi?"

She took a deep breath. "I am a princess. My tree, along with nineteen others, live in a circle around the manifestation."

"What is the manifestation?"

"A flame. I've never had to explain it before. The Heart of our world lives in this forest. I am connected to it, literally. My roots grow inside it. It blesses me with life when I sacrifice to it. That's why a Verdant must be pure. We sacrifice. The manifestation shows us how the Heart is feeling by the color the flame burns. It is so beautiful, Ler. I wish I could show it to you."

"Why can't you?"

"Umm...I'm sure it's not allowed. I haven't told anyone about meeting you." Shi visibly shivered. "It's my secret."

He frowned and crossed his arms over his chest.

"What's wrong?"

"I don't like the sound of this Verdant stuff."

"Why?"

He turned his back and paced for a moment. "I'm going to try to be as honest with you as I can. I don't like it because I want you free, and you're not. I want your heart to be open to my advances and free to accept them. You said you're a princess. I know something of that because I'm the king."

"The king of the vampires?"

"No. I'm the king of all of Regia. Every race is subject to me, even yours."

Shi looked perplexed, then her eyes widened. "What are you going to do to my people?"

"What?"

She shook her head and backed away. "You're planning something aren't you? You want to take over us, force us to change, move us away from the Heart."

"No, Shi. I'm not planning...I would never hurt you."

"No, I don't believe you. You're planning something." She turned and ran.

Leramiun ran after her, catching her from behind. She struggled.

"Shh..." he soothed. "You're right. I am planning something."

"What?" she demanded, turning to face him.

He cupped her face. "I'm planning to kiss you again."

She went rigid but made no attempt to escape his grasp. "You must not," she whispered. "It's forbidden."

"We're royalty, Shi. That should amount to something. Give us power and freedom to do as we please."

He ran his thumb along her trembling lower lip. "I've thought about you non-stop since last night. I've fantasized about what I want to do with you. Please, let me kiss you. I've already kissed you. What difference does it make if it happens again?"

"I don't know."

"Just a kiss. Nothing more."

"Such things are not for me. I don't know or understand these things. I'm not even supposed to see others engaging in...affection."

"I could teach you."

Shi trembled with the inexplicable urge to cry and shook her head.

He let go of her. "There's nothing I wouldn't give you, Shi. Nothing I wouldn't do for you. Will you leave me no hope at all?"

"It is as you said. I am not free."

He could see she was about to flee from him.

"I'll be here tomorrow night...waiting for you. I'll come every night for the rest of my life for just the chance of seeing you again."

"Goodbye," she gasped, and ran while she still had the strength to resist him.

He took in a ragged breath as he watched her go, not moving until the glow of her was swallowed completely by the night.

It wasn't over, not by a long shot.

Leramiun decided he needed a little walk to clear his head before he headed home and let his body relax. He didn't pay attention to his direction, just walking, lost again in fantasies. He toyed with the End of the Bridge, rolling it around and around in his hand. Time didn't matter to him. He'd take as much time as he desired. He wandered, directionless. As the predawn grayed the sky, a bad smell broke through the fog in his head, and he tripped and fell face first over a dead body.

Leramiun scrambled to his feet. Bones and body parts twisted and stuck up like a macabre garden. The hairs on the back of his neck stood up. It made no sense, even though he knew it existed; his mind rejected what he saw. There had been no battle. None of the dead here had died at the same time, each in a different state of decomposition. No weapons littered the ground. Not one was dressed for battle. No, this was nothing but a dumping ground.

He fought his desire to crush the End of the Bridge and forced himself to stay. Who would do such a thing? What for? A thought clicked firmly into place in his mind as he remembered the feeling of warning near those monumental trees. But he knew now they weren't mere trees. And they guarded something priceless.

Rage filled him as he looked on the victims. The Dryads would answer for this. And as he exacted judgment on them for the dead, he'd take his own price from them. They would give Shi up to him or he'd kill them all.

CHAPTER 5

Leramiun slept late into the morning. Helena lay tucked in beside him. He ignored her completely, doing everything not to touch her in the slightest way. When he finally dragged himself out of bed, Helena was dressed and sitting in the corner, reading again.

"Good morning, Your Highness," she said sweetly, too sweetly.

Leramiun grunted and rubbed the sleep from his eyes. "You don't have to stay here, now. Go about whatever it is you do."

She didn't move. He looked at her, and the expression on her face brought him fully awake.

"But, what about what you promised me? I've kept your confidence."

"Right. That. I'll honor my word to you. But I have a lot to do today."

"Fine. I'll just stay right here as you requested."

"Helena, I don't need you to--"

A sharp knock on the door interrupted him.

"It's Quinn," his brother said through the door. "Open up."

Leramiun shot her a stern glance before opening the door.

Quinn surveyed his bother with a mocking smile. "You look terrible. What has that whore done to you?"

"What do you want, Quinn?"

"Just a little brotherly concern," Quinn said. "Haven't seen you around. You know, walking the halls with your *I'm the king* look on your face."

Leramiun punched Quinn in the arm. "All right, sucker. I'm fine. I'll see you later."

He shut the door. Helena looked at him expectantly. He sighed. "Stay here today, if you like. I'll be busy."

"Yes, sire."

He could tell she was upset, but he didn't have the energy to do anything about it right now. He went to bathe and get dressed for his day. His mind torn between thoughts of Shi and the mass grave, he didn't know what to do about either. He was determined not to make a mistake, it was too important.

He ate a late breakfast, listening to the chatter of his advisors around the table with more interest than usual. More than once, he almost spilled about the mass grave and his discovery of a new race, but decided he needed to wait just a little longer.

****

The day held no joy for Shi. She walked among her kind, staying close to the flame, filled with a constant caress of desolation. She sat on the ground, starring into the flame, and seeing only Ler.

"Shi? Shi! What are you doing?" Mae's voice ruptured the sad silence inside her.

She looked up at Mae standing next to her. "Nothing."

"Yes, I can see that. Why are you doing nothing? It's preparation day."

Shi looked around, suddenly very alert. "Preparation day? Are you sure?"

Mae gazed at her in disbelief. "Of course I'm sure. Can't you hear it?"

She could hear it now. All the other Verdant had started singing, the song moving through the wood, getting all the Dryads in the right mindset for their seclusion as the equinox came upon them. Shi scrambled to her feet, raising her voice in the song. Mae nodded in approval and walked away, singing as well.

Shi smiled at everyone she passed, continuing to sing. All the Verdant spread out, so that no one was unaware of the day or what they were getting ready for. Shi's desolation came back. She tried not to let it show. She'd forgotten about preparation, so she hadn't told Ler that she couldn't come meet him. A wave of fear rolled over her. Seclusion lasted two nights. What if, after waiting for her and she didn't show up, he never came back at all?

The thought choked her, and she couldn't sing for a moment. She continued walking out toward the edge, trying to free the notes lodged in her throat. She wasn't trying to sneak up on anyone, or overhear anything. But the deep tones of Elder Fer stopped her in her tracks.

"Are you finished?"

"Almost, sir," another replied.

Shi peeked around the corner. Elder Fer talked to a warrior. She took a step back and held still, listening.

"Good. Make sure you don't place the bodies too close. We don't want that smell here."

"Yes. Have no fear. By tonight, the smell of death will protect our borders."

"I hate this time of year. Two nights of seclusion! Two nights of leaving our people unguarded."

"I know, sir. I hate it, too."

Shi listened, but they said nothing else. What bodies were they talking about? Who had the warriors killed and why? Could it be that they were so determined to keep their privacy they killed those who threatened it? Was that why she had never seen any but her own kind? A chill spread through her. Would they hurt Ler? Yes, she felt sure they would, for touching her, if nothing else.

Indignation rose inside her as her suspicions grew. She continued in her work of uplifting everyone around her with song, the notes came out now without her having to think of them. A dangerous *what if* sprang to life like a spark in her mind, and by the evening it had grown into a healthy fire.

Shi went to see Shea before the equinox ceremony began, but as she approached her sister's place, she stopped abruptly. Hul was wrapped around Shea, kissing her passionately. Shi watched for a moment, she'd never seen him be quite so...much before. She noticed Shea's altered breathing and the way her hands clenched and pulled him closer.

Shi turned around and went back to the flame.

The equinox ceremony was the same every time. Everyone gathered in a circle around the Heart at the onset of night. The Verdant began singing again, the notes falling gently on everyone's ears. No one spoke. When the song was over, the root chalice, filled with the drugged sap wine, passed from person to person. Everyone took one sip then went back to their trees, climbed inside, and instantly fell asleep. The elders drank first. Then the breeders, the warriors, and last, the Verdant. Shi had carefully chosen the last place. Mae took her drink and passed the chalice to Shi. Shi looked at Mae. Mae's eyes glazed over, and she walked to her tree and climbed inside. Shi looked down at the last little bit of wine and poured it out on the ground. She set the chalice carefully by her tree.

A chill swept over her. She was all alone. No protection. No eyes on her. No one to stop her. She was free...if only for two days and nights. The entire world could exist in two days.

****

Leramiun sensed something was amiss as soon as the End of the Bridge dumped him on the ground. He walked a little in the darkness, scanning the area, listening carefully. As he approached the massive line of trees, the stench of death stopped him dead in his tracks. His pulse jumped violently. *Shi!* Was she okay? Logic pushed its way through his initial panic, and he took a deep breath of the vile smell. It was old. No one who died in the last few days would smell like that. Plus, it was a smell he recognized, werewolf.

Vexed over the stench, but nonetheless relieved, he moved off, away from the smell, back to where he'd first laid eyes on her, and waited. He didn't have to wait long. He felt her coming before he saw her. An intense energy radiated from her. She walked toward him in a rush, her beauty almost bringing him to his knees. Before he could even say hello, she grabbed his hand.

"Come with me," she whispered.

Gladly, anywhere, he thought as she pulled him forward. He didn't hesitate or even notice where she was leading him, all he could perceive was their hands entwined and the amazing sensation her skin rubbed onto his. She pulled him past the rotting smell, past the monumental trees, and into a dream. She stopped and turned to look at him. "They sleep. All of them. No one knows you're here. No one will harm you."

He smiled. "Really? *You* won't harm me?"

She looked genuinely confused.

He chuckled and rubbed the heel of his hand over his heart. "I'll risk any further damage, but you've already dealt me a mortal wound, Shi. My heart's broken beyond all hope."

She put her hand over his and looked deep in his eyes. "You say the strangest things...and I think maybe you say them to achieve something, though I don't know what. But still, your words come back to me when I'm alone. I hear your voice when I'm not with you, and I look at your face even when my eyes are closed. Why is that?"

His expression became entirely serious. "It is the same with me."

"You hardly know anything about me."

"That changes nothing."

"I hardly know anything about you."

"I'll tell you anything you want to know," he said.

She opened her mouth then snapped it shut, shaking her head. "No, I ask too many questions."

He frowned. "Shi, ask me anything. I want you to."

"No. Time is too short. I wanted to show you the manifestation. It's more striking in the dark, the same is true of the waterfalls."

She laced her fingers through his and led him into the thick of the wood.

Leramiun found it hard to breathe as he stood on the shore gazing at the waterfall. Had he not met Shi before seeing it, he would have insisted such natural beauty could not exist. The light coming from the water had hypnotic power, but he couldn't stand to look at anything too long while Shi was next to him. Her beauty was more hypnotic than the water.

Then she led him to the manifestation. He saw the white flames in the distance and felt such a pull of power through his whole body, he ran, pulling her along, desperate to see, desperate to absorb more.

"Careful," she cautioned. "Approach slowly."

"Can I touch it?"

"No, you must not. Only the Verdant are allowed."

He watched the sensual dance of the flames. They shot out of the ground but consumed nothing. No heat came from them.

"The Heart of the world lies here, just under our feet. The flames are the outpouring of the Heart's emotions. It is my job, along with the other Verdant, to minister to the flame."

Leramiun tore his eyes away reluctantly. He understood the mass grave. He understood why the Dryads held a line they allowed no one to cross. But who gave them the authority to claim ownership? If this truly was the Heart of Regia, then it should belong to everyone. It should belong to him. He was the king after all.

He turned his full attention back to Shi. "Which one is you?"

She laid a hand on the tree next to her. "This one."

He looked up into the canopy. It was an undeniably odd moment. He reached out and laid his hand flat against the trunk. Shi shivered.

"You feel that?"

She giggled nervously. "I do. I had no idea that I would."

A devious glint lit his eyes.

"Don't get any ideas," she threatened.

"But that's what I do when I'm with you. I get ideas."

Shi looked at him fearfully. He pulled his hand away.

"Well, you're a beautiful...tree, as well as a beautiful woman."

"I didn't know if I should show you or not. I thought it might be too much, just how different we really are from each other. I thought it might scare you away."

"And you don't want to scare me away?"

"No," she whispered.

He felt her eyes go straight to his heart and pin it.

"Gah!" He threw his hands up and walked away. "What are you doing to me?"

"What?" She chased after him.

"I don't know why I come here, eagerly wanting this torture... I should go before it's too late."

"Too late for what?"

He stopped and looked at the ground. "I'm a bastard. It doesn't matter what this will do to my heart, but yours... When I kissed you, you said I had no right. I still don't. And what I've been doing... It's working. I'm wearing down your defenses."

"Why?"

He laughed darkly. "Because I want you—" He looked up then, his eyes swallowing her. "Do you understand?"

"No! I don't understand!" she cried. "Sometimes I think I'm starting to comprehend. You've changed things for me since I first saw you. I was so alone. I didn't realize how much I resented my position. I didn't choose the life I lead. And no one can touch me; everyone treats me as though I have no feelings. I'm above them, too fragile for real life. And then I break one rule and go out beyond the boundary and there you are. You don't treat me the way they do..."

He placed both hands gently on her cheeks. "I'm lost, Shi. I'm totally lost in you, and I don't know what to do about it."

She looked at her hands, surprised to see them clenched on his shoulders. She recognized the tension, remembering the way her sister's hands looked earlier that day. She looked back into the depths of his azure eyes and realized she was caught in the undertow.

"Remember the things I told you I'm not supposed to know?"

He sighed and dropped his hands. "Yes. I remember."

He made to turn away, but she held fast to his shirt. He looked back at her quizzically.

Her whole body trembled. "Teach me."

His mouth fell open in shock, then slowly, very slowly, his lips curved into a smile.

Calm down, he told himself. *Use your head.*

Taking a deep breath, Leramiun reached down and picked her up. She clung around his neck, her gaze frightened but determined. He looked for a nice soft place to set her down, but he was suddenly acutely aware they were surrounded by other people. Trees would have never tamped down his passion before, but now...he wanted way more privacy than this. Shi said they were sleeping. Sleeping or not, he felt exposed.

He carried her out of the dense area back toward the waterfall. The trees cleared around the beach. That was better. Then, he had another problem. What did he really plan to do with her? She gave him an open invitation to something that was totally foreign to her. Hell, there might be more than a few differences in the way vampires went about this compared to Dryads.

He looked back in her eyes and felt himself crumble. He couldn't throw her on the ground and have his way with her. She wasn't a whore from his harem. She was the most innocent person he'd ever met. He wouldn't betray her trust like that.

He set her down gently and sat in the sand next to her. She looked confused.

"All right. You can't learn everything at one time," he said, smiling. "And it's important that you know a vampire's mouth is the most sensitive place on their whole body."

She smirked at him. "When I said teach me, I thought you'd take a more *hands on* approach."

"Shh! You're the student."

She straightened up and placed her hands in her lap, trying to look serious.

"My fangs can break the skin with the slightest pressure. I could easily lose my head with your blood in my mouth. Understand?"

She raised one eyebrow and nodded.

"Now, student, after what you've just learned, think carefully about how you would like to kiss me...then proceed to practical application."

Shi snorted. If that's how he wanted to play, she was game. She leaned toward him then stopped. "Close your eyes," she said.

He smiled and obeyed. She gazed at him and waited for his face to relax. Then she lifted her hand and ran her fingers along the side of his face, and then very lightly across his lips. His mouth parted, and his breath blew out raggedly over her finger. She didn't need to think about this. She'd thought about it over and over again since that first night.

Shi wet her lips and pressed them against his. He moaned as if he was in some wonderful agony. She moved her lips and pressed them harder. His hand came up and braced on her shoulder. She could feel the level of power she had over him and decided to push him further. She sucked his bottom lip hard into her mouth and bit down on it.

Leramiun jolted, his eyes flying open in shock. Shi pulled back from him.

"You..." he panted. "Did you forget what I told you about my mouth?!"

"No. I didn't forget," she said, smiling sweetly.

His eyes widened at her. "You're a bad girl!"

She raised her eyebrows and laughed.

"Will you be my queen?"

Shi stopped laughing. "What did you say?"

He brought her hand to his lips and kissed it. "Will you be my queen?"

Shi frowned and looked out at the water.

Her frown made his heart plummet. "Shi, please. I have to have you for myself. I can't choose a bride off a damn list, not now." He thought of Helena and all the other women he'd been with casually. "And I can't treat you like a whore."

Her eyes cut back to him. "Do you love me?"

He gulped. "I think I do. I know it's too fast to seem real."

A sob rose up Shi's chest. "I don't know if what I feel for you is love, but it's strong... When I think of you, I feel more than I ever have. It aches, it whispers, and it sings. I hoped you would love me. I want you to." She abruptly looked away, pain pulling down on her face. "I shouldn't want your love. It's wrong."

"What difference does it make whether you want it or not? Because you'll have it regardless. Please say you'll be mine."

She looked back at him, a strong questioning in her eyes.

"Are you worried about...you know...children?" he asked.

Shi smiled and shook her head. "Not at all. I can't have any. My womb was removed from me when I was a baby, after my mother decided I would become a Verdant."

"Ler? What's wrong?"

His eyes had gone wide and their blue froze. He took her hand in a firm but shaking grip. "Shi, come away with me... Come away... Leave these *cruel* people behind."

"I can't go anywhere. I'm bound to my tree."

"Then I'll uproot you. I'll have you transplanted to the castle's garden. I'll take care of you. Protect you."

"Not possible. My roots grow inside the Heart. To remove them would kill me."

Leramiun put his head in his hands and pinched his eyes shut.

"Maybe this is all the time we can have," she said sadly. "Just two nights. There's too much to overcome. We aren't meant to be, Ler. We're too different."

"Do you want to be my queen or not?"

"Of course I do."

"Then you will be, and that's all there is to it. We'll figure it out. Change was coming anyway."

"What do you mean?"

He looked back into her eyes and touched her cheek. "I have something hard to tell you. There's been a terrible crime committed by some of your people. As the king, I have to do something about it."

"The warriors have killed?"

"How do you know about it?"

She shrugged. "I overheard some of them talking earlier today. They talked about moving bodies to protect us while we slept. That's all I know."

"I need your help, Shi. I have to be sure. Will you come with me? It's going to be *unpleasant*. If I showed you the dead, would you be able to tell for sure that your warriors killed them?"

"I believe so."

He led her out past the sleeping warriors, gently but possessively holding her hand. They passed close to one of the moved bodies.

"Ugh." Shi covered her nose and looked at the decaying corpse. "What is that?"

"A werewolf."

"Werewolf?"

"I'll tell you about them later. They are a strong and interesting people, even though they cause me tons of trouble."

Shi knew she was about to see more things she didn't want to see, but she continued to let Ler lead her. The pull began in her back, letting her know she was getting close to the end of her invisible tether.

"I can't go much farther."

"We're almost there. Look, that way." He pointed.

Shi walked as far as she could go and stopped. She clung to Ler's arm and stared, transfixed and horrified. Tears welled up and slid freely down her cheeks.

"It's not right," she whispered. "Their loved ones don't know where they are. The dead are not honored by this. Each one of them had a name."

"Did the Dryad warriors do this?"

Shi nodded. "This was as far as they could go. What threat could these people have posed to us?"

"I have to do something, Shi. It's my responsibility."

"What are you going to do?"

"I'm going to have to contemplate what justice should be. I promise I shall not be hasty in my decision. But the time of Dryad seclusion is over... Come on, let's go back."

"Wait, just a moment," she said, taking a step away from him.

It was his turn to be transfixed. Shi kneeled down and placed both her hands flat on the ground. She closed her eyes and exhaled deeply. A surge of light came out of her hands and ran along the ground toward the dead. Flowers sprang up where the light had been, blossoming in a ring around the grave.

She stood up and took his hand again. She shrugged as he gaped at her. "It's the only thing I can do right now to honor them."

"You're so beautiful...in every way."

CHAPTER 6

Leramiun slunk inside Quinn's darkened bedroom. His pulse hammered in his veins with excitement. He ran to Quinn's sleeping form and began shaking him. He woke up swearing and swung a punch at Leramiun's face. He ducked and caught the edge of Quinn's knuckles on the side of his head.

"SHH! Shut up!" Leramiun said, blocking Quinn's fist again. "Get up and get dressed quickly. I need your help."

Quinn yawned and made a quick assessment of the manic light in Leramiun's eyes. "Geez, what's with you?"

Leramiun smiled and went to Quinn's closet, grabbing a handful of clothes, and threw them on the bed next to his brother. "I need you to come and witness for me."

Quinn blinked a few times then laughed aloud.

"Shh!"

"I'm sorry, but what mind altering substance have you been consuming?"

Leramiun knelt next to his brother's bed and grabbed his hand desperately. "I'm in love. I have to finalize everything with Shi in secret. Now, as the sun rises. It has to be now, before anyone can stop it. The ritual won't be legitimate unless there's a witness. I need your help. Please, Quinn! Do this for me. I'm asking as your brother. I can't trust anyone else with this."

Quinn shook his head, exasperated, and reached for the clothes next to him. "Shi? That's a name I certainly don't recognize. She must really be something for all this...drama. I thought you were besotted with that whore squatting in your bedroom."

Leramiun wasn't really listening. He paced as Quinn got dressed.

"All right. Am I presentable?"

"Yes, yes," Leramiun said, not even glancing at Quinn.

"Do you have the royal signet dagger?" Quinn asked.

"Of course. Are you ready?"

"As ready as I'll ever be to see you engage in total lunacy and put your throne in jeopardy."

"There's no danger of that. Shi's a princess."

Leramiun smashed another End of the Bridge between his hands and pulled Quinn with him into its rushing darkness. They landed in the sand by the silver waterfall. Quinn brushed the sand from his boots, stood upright, and stared open mouthed at the water.

"Whoa! Did we just go off world?"

Leramiun smiled and slapped Quinn on the shoulder. "No."

"Where are we? Why haven't I been here before if this is Regia?"

"I didn't know about it either until a few days ago. Magnificent isn't it? It's been hidden and protected for a very long time."

"By whom?"

"Dryads. Imagine it, Quinn! I've discovered a Regian race that has lived here and thrived right under our noses. They've been a total law unto themselves. But that's about to change. They're the ones responsible for the mass grave that was recently discovered."

Quinn looked at his brother quizzically. "O-kay," he said slowly. "What does that have to do with you dragging me out here in the middle of the night for some woman?"

"Shi is a Dryad. She can't travel very far from this place, and really, there's no place as beautiful as this for our ceremony."

Quinn chuckled and shook his head. "You've lost your mind. I don't care if she is a real princess. You're choosing a bride of another race! That's going to go over really well with the people. Not to mention your Halfling children. I mean, really, how can this...Leramiun? What are you staring at?"

Quinn followed his brother's wide-eyed line of sight and felt himself winded as he laid eyes on Shi.

"Okay, I get it," he whispered. "Does she have a sister?"

Leramiun didn't answer. He rushed at Shi, scooped her up, and spun her in a circle. "I missed you."

"You were only gone a few moments," she laughed. "But I missed you, too."

She looked at Quinn. He felt his stomach drop and his cheeks burn.

"Is this your brother?"

"Yes." Leramiun led Shi by the hand over to Quinn.

"Shi, this is my younger brother, Quinn. Quinn, this is Shi."

She smiled and gave him a small bow. "Thank you for coming."

Quinn felt dizzy looking at her. "I...uh...anything for your happiness. I mean, you're welcome."

She looked openly at him for a moment, her friendly smile slipping. Her black iridescent eyes tunneling down into his. Shi flinched and took a step closer to Leramiun, grabbing hold of his arm.

"The sun will be rising. Are you ready?" Shi asked Leramiun.

He laughed and kissed her hand. "Do you need to ask? You're not worried about the ceremony, are you? I promise it won't be that painful."

"No. I'm not worried."

****

Shi shook the chill Quinn gave her and focused on what she was about to do. The sun began its ascension, casting shimmering light rays on the waterfall. The water in turn bounced it back around them. She faced Ler and held his hands. She felt no fear, had no hesitation. He'd been clearly nervous when he'd described the ritual to her earlier, but the idea didn't bother her at all. She thought it was beautiful.

Ler looked at her so intently. She held her breath as he began to speak.

"I choose you, Shi, Verdant princess of the Dryads, to be my queen. I vow from this moment, until I take my last breath, no other woman shall have my tender thoughts. No other woman shall have my heart, my soul, or my bed. Everything I am is solely yours, if you will accept and be mine."

His words sent a rush through her; a single tear ran down her cheek.

"I accept. And I vow to you, Leramiun, King of Regia, that from this moment, until I take my last breath, you have my heart. From now on I am no longer a Verdant, I am only your queen, if you accept."

"I accept."

Ler let go of her hands and pulled a dagger from his belt. Shi squared her shoulders and nodded in encouragement. He drew the length of the blade diagonally across his palm, his blood falling on the sand. He handed her the blade. Shi took a deep breath and copied him, her golden blood surging up from the wound. Quinn stepped forward and took the dagger.

Shi held out her wounded hand to Ler. He covered her wound with his, and their blood mixed together.

"As we shed our blood together, our vows are struck. In this symbol, you know that I will die before I fail to fulfill my vow to you." He looked at her intently, and she repeated his words.

"I will die before I fail to fulfill my vow to you."

They separated their hands, scars now replaced the wounds. His was a golden line, hers red.

A current of energy welled up inside her at the thought of what she'd just done and what she now was, and she threw her arms around his neck and kissed him.

Ler tossed an End of the Bridge at Quinn. "Thanks, Quinn. See yourself home will you?"

Shi glanced at Ler's brother and quickly looked away. She wanted him gone as soon as possible. There was something wrong behind his eyes. She didn't want to look in them again. He was like a shadow crouching on the fringe of her happiness.

Quinn didn't linger. The portal absorbed him and closed, leaving the king and queen alone.

****

Ler was very patient and slow as he taught her many new things that warm golden morning. She climbed each new level of sensation with trust and enthusiasm. He seemed at ease until the moment he sank his teeth into her shoulder. Shi felt a sliver of her life force leave her body and run into him.

He pulled away, her blood on his lips, his head thrown back, and his eyes clenched shut. For a second Shi worried she'd somehow hurt him. The veins in his neck throbbed, and his body trembled with some invisible strain. Ler took a deep breath and opened his eyes. Shi gasped. His eyes burned wild and ravenous.

But Shi learned a loss of control had its own rewards. The day blossomed beautifully exhausting.

Chapter 7

Quinn deliberately brought himself back to the Onyx castle right inside Leramiun's bedchambers. His brother's whore slept in the middle of the bed, undisturbed by the lateness of the morning. He felt oddly suspended above the floor. New jealousy layered over his old jealousy, creeping and slithering into his inmost parts, poisoning him irrevocably. He couldn't swallow this. Leramiun couldn't have all the power, the throne, *and* Shi.

He thought of her, rage burning him up inside. He understood his brother's action. Had he seen her first she would be his and not Leramiun's. She tipped the scales, forcing him into action. Quinn's ears rang, his perception closing down, as his hands sought something to destroy. No one responded to Helena's screams.

When his rage ran its course and he came back to himself, his hands were blood covered. He knelt over Helena's crumpled frame and felt for a pulse. She was alive, barely. Sighing angrily, Quinn cut his wrist on his teeth and shoved the wound into her mouth. As soon as she came around, he pulled his arm away from her.

It was only a small prod at his brother, but he'd have to settle for small strikes. At least for now. Quinn picked her up, carried her to his room, and dumped her on the bed.

Her eyelids fluttered, and she moaned in pain. He snapped his fingers loudly next to her face. She looked at him and tried to pull away, terrified.

"You're my property now, whore. This room is your whole world. If I catch you trying to leave, I'll cut off your feet."

After changing out of his bloody clothes, Quinn set out to find his friends. They would spread the gossip he was about to give them through the castle faster than wildfire. But as he came out into the hall, he was nearly smashed by one of his father's oldest advisors, huffing as he ran.

"Hey!" Quinn yelled.

The old man skidded to a halt and rushed back to Quinn, grabbing him by the arms. "Where's the king?! Where is Leramiun?!"

"He's not here. What's going on?"

"Come on, sire!" The advisor pulled him forward. "Fortress' special forces are here. A portal has been opened from a new world, and a *person* has come through."

"So what?" Quinn demanded. "We open portals and go to other worlds all the time."

"Yes! *We!* We open them! This portal was opened on the other world. And this one who has come through has great power. He calls himself a wizard. We need Leramiun to decide what we are going to do about this."

Quinn smiled. He practically skipped to the council chambers where everyone was in a panic. Fortress' group of elite stood in the back, along the wall, waiting for some order. Some looked at him when he came in and nodded a half bow. Quinn took his chance and sat down in Leramiun's place. Everyone looked at him then.

"Sit down!" he commanded the room.

Everyone sat.

"Sire, by what authority have you taken your brother's place?"

"His," Quinn said easily. "My brother is not in the castle at present. He has run off to mate the bride of his choice and won't be back for a little while yet. I am the prince, and while he is away, I will stand in his stead... So, we have a problem. Tell me about this *wizard*."

Quinn's info bomb caused a new panic that redirected the conversation for quite a while.

****

Shi leaned her back against her trunk and stared into the flame. She was changed; different than she had been the night before. Her people were going to have a hard time accepting this, but they would, so long as she had proof the Heart accepted it. Shi took a deep breath. Moment of truth.

She bowed before the manifestation and put her hands in the flame. For a moment, she felt nothing. Then the flame tickled her new scar, sank into it, explored it. She waited, holding totally still. It didn't bless her, but it didn't reject her either. Shi felt a soft surge into her hands and a knowledge run into her roots. The Heart still loved her. She had saddened it, but it accepted her choice.

Shi walked back to where Ler waited for her. Worry pulled on his beautiful face. She sank into his strong arms and sighed. "It's all right. The Heart accepts us."

They held tightly to each other, feeling the stress of the moment leave them.

"The evening is upon us," Ler said seriously.

"Yes. And when the morning dawns, everyone will wake, and I'll have to tell them. You have to go back to your people and tell them as well."

"Yeah, it's going to be a long day tomorrow."

"What's going to happen?"

"Well, what do you think if I built a house here? I wouldn't be able to be here all the time, but here with you would be my home, and all the rest would just be my work."

Shi's smile warmed his heart. "That sounds good. It'll have to be a small house, though. Nothing big like you're used to."

"That's fine. Just something for us to have some privacy."

He laced his fingers through hers and looked at her seriously. "This is going to be hard, you know."

"What is?"

"Us. We won't be accepted by the people. Our peace, when we have it, will always be short lived."

"If you're trying to scare me away, you're too late." She held up her scarred palm. "And, so far, of the two of us, I'm the one who's taken all the risks...and that short lived peace you just mentioned, we have some right now. And you're wasting it with all your talk."

He chuckled. She was right, of course. And apparently she hadn't found the consummating of their relationship unpleasant.

He ran the tip of his nose up the side of her neck, inhaling deeply. Even her scent seemed imbued with life. He gently ran his fingers through her hair, gathering it together, and draped it over her other shoulder, giving him more access to her skin.

Shi's bottom lip trembled involuntarily as he pressed a kiss just under her ear.

"Since what we did earlier." Her voice came out weak. "And I understand what will come next if you keep that up, I was just...wondering,"

"What?"

"Well, I warned you I'm curious. Was that all? Or do you have more to teach?"

He looked at her with wide eyes, clearly and pleasantly shocked. He'd pulled out every bedroom trick in his whole repartee earlier. And she wanted more?!

"Uh...sure there's more."

"Really? You don't sound too confident."

"I'll make something up."

Shi found Ler's improvisation delightful, except that one thing, which they both agreed never to mention again.

****

Ler's heart ached as he left Shi. But the sooner he took care of business, the sooner he'd have her in his arms again. The End of the Bridge pulled him from paradise and dropped him back in dreary real life.

"I'm back, Helena," he said before his eyes adjusted to the dimness of his bedchamber. "Helena? Are you..."

The room was in shambles. The bed looked like a troop of ogres had walked over it. Bedding was flung all around the room. His chair was turned on its side, and there was blood on the floor. Leramiun went out into the hall, looking for answers. Despite the earliness of the hour, voices he recognized drifted down the hall, in heated debate. He walked to the council chambers and stood in the doorway, shocked as he watched and listened.

All of his advisors were there. Everyone looked tired except Quinn. Quinn looked vibrant and pleased, and he was sitting in *his* chair.

"What's going on here?" Leramiun demanded loudly, striding into the room.

"Oh, sire, you're back! Thank goodness!"

Everyone began speaking at once, except Quinn who looked sullen. Leramiun stood next to his chair and held up his hands.

"One at a time!"

His oldest advisor told him all about the portal and the wizard, who was currently the guest of Fortress. "And we didn't know where you were! Nothing would have been accomplished had Quinn not taken charge. And he tells us you've gone off and chosen your queen! Is this so?"

Leramiun looked down at his brother pointedly. Quinn shrugged, got up, and took his usual seat.

"Thank you all for doing your jobs while I was away, and for listening to Quinn's voice as though it were my own. I am putting him in charge of the issue with this wizard...but I am to be alerted immediately when anything new arises with this. You say he's harmed no one?"

"No, sire. And he came alone as an ambassador. He says they seek asylum."

"All right. Then I shall direct your attention on to the other matter of my queen, the discovery of her race, and the justice we will be bringing to those who created the mass grave."

****

Shi had never felt so afraid. She knew she'd never had a better reason for fear. Everyone began to wake up. They all looked refreshed and peaceful. Mae approached her, smiling. Shi clenched her hands tight as Mae grasped her arms in a friendly, brisk way.

"Good morning, Shi! What a beautiful beginning to the new equinox. Wouldn't you agree? Shi? What's wrong with you?"

Shi braced herself. "I need to speak to the elders. Will you go and tell them? I have important news."

"What is this news?"

Shi shook her head. "I have to tell the elders first."

Mae looked irritated, but she nodded and walked away. Shi only had a few moments, and she realized she needed to see Shea before she shook everyone's world to pieces. She ran to her sister's place.

Shea had just climbed out of her trunk and was yawning. Hul was standing behind her, rubbing her shoulders.

"Shea!" Shi ran to her sister and grasped her in a tight hug.

"Shi, what's wrong?"

Shi pulled back. "I'm scared, Shea. I'm afraid of what the elders will do to me when they see this."

Shi held her palm up for her sister to see her red scar. Shea looked at it, clearly confused.

"It's a mating scar, Shea... I'm in love."

"What?!" Shea exclaimed.

"Shhh."

"What's happening?" Hul asked, leaning over Shea's shoulder to see Shi's hand.

"Shi's been defiled!" Shea told Hul.

"Don't say that! It's not ugly. I made a choice. The Heart accepts it. It accepts me and Ler."

"Ler? Who's Ler?" Hul demanded. His eyes swept over her, landing on her shoulder where Ler's bite still shone on her skin. "Oh no!" he breathed, looking seriously at Shea. "Our borders have been breached. I have to warn the elders!"

"Wait! I told Mae to tell the elders I needed to talk them. I'm going to tell them everything."

Hul snarled in her face. "You don't understand anything! You're just a sheltered Verdant who's been victimized, too stupid to know you've let the enemy in."

"No, you don't understand!" Shi yelled.

Hul slapped her. Shock spun inside her as she fell to the ground, her face on fire with pain. She looked up, tears blurring her vision. Shea had grabbed him by the arm and pulled him back.

"Hul, stop!" Shea pleaded.

He took a deep breath and placed his hands on her pregnant belly. "I'm just afraid for our family."

Then he strode off, raising the alarm as he went. Shi's fear turned into a cold, white panic as she was surrounded by her people. She found herself alone, their scared, angry gazes forming an ocean around her. Elders Fer and Pru came to the forefront of the people.

They moved slowly toward her, one on each side. Their wrinkled hands grasped at her. Fer touched her bite mark, and Pru examined her red scar. They exchanged meaningful looks.

"Let's go to the Heart," Fer said to everyone.

The elders pulled her along as the entire group headed to the Heart.

Both elders examined her tree closely. "She has not been rejected," Pru declared.

Pru gave her a soft look. "Don't worry, Shi. Nothing is your fault. Just tell us what happened."

Anger, as she had never experienced it, shot through her body. She straightened her shoulders and lifted her head, returning the condemning stares of her people with outrage.

"Nothing is my fault?" she repeated. "That's certainly true! If *you* didn't kill innocent people and dump their bodies in a shameful pile in the forest, we wouldn't be having this conversation!"

Both elders blinked at her, clearly shocked. "How do you know about that?" Fer demanded.

"We do what we have to, to protect the Heart and our people," Pru insisted.

"Well, you're about to answer for it! And you better be careful how you treat me, all of you. Leramiun, *King* Leramiun, will be very displeased when he learns what you've put his queen through."

Shi marched to the flame and put her hand in it to prove her point. "I am not rejected! And the vampires are coming. Get used to it. Everything is about to change."

****

It was an even longer and even more arduous meeting than he had anticipated. Everyone was upset by his news. Leramiun realized he should have known how thrown off balance they would be and just how long it would take them to accept it.

"Sire, if you truly intend to set up a residence there, so close to the Lair, I must insist you have security established."

"The point is to be private. The werewolves won't know I'm there," he argued.

"But *if* they learned, your life would be threatened every time you went there. And your queen. She would be in danger of being used as leverage against you."

"No, that can't happen!" Quinn interjected loudly. Everyone looked at him. He blushed brightly. "They're right, Brother. Protection must be in place."

Leramiun sighed, seeing they were right. "What should I do? The Dryad warriors have been effective protectors, albeit misguided."

"You must have a guard, sire."

"That's not enough," Quinn said. "A handful of royal soldiers can't stand up to an onslaught of wolves."

"What about the sand?" Leramiun asked. "We could bring it in and run it around the outside of the Dryad's area."

Everyone looked around at each other nodding in approval. "That would be effective, sire. When shall we begin bringing it?"

"Tomorrow." Leramiun stood up and stretched. "Now we go to exact judgment for the innocent dead. Prepare the Crimson Brotherhood. Today they carry axes, not swords."

CHAPTER 8

It was out of her hands. Shi sat next to her trunk and waited for Ler to come. She was the only Dryad who was able to be still. Everyone else was in a tizzy. The warriors prepared for battle at the prompting of the elders, despite what she said. The breeders moved back and forth, talking non-stop, and the Verdant huddled together, trying to cope with the bursting of their sheltered bubble. And Shi was alone. But strangely, she didn't feel as alone as she used to. Her memories of Ler came back to her like a series of bright flashes. She gently ran her fingers over the ridges of his bite mark and smiled to herself.

She rested her head back and realized just how tired she was. She hadn't slept in such a long time. Shi dozed off in the afternoon sunlight.

Yelling and the scuffle of running feet jostled her awake. Shi got quickly to her feet, her heart in her throat. Beyond the sound that woke her came the vibrations through the ground, shaking her roots. She ran to see, but as she pushed through the crowd, a strong arm wrapped around her, lifting her off the ground, and hauled her back.

Shocked, she looked up into the face of Ree. "Not you," he said roughly. "The enemy can't have you."

"They aren't our enemies!"

Ree snorted derisively. Shi kicked and scratched at him. He quickly wound a vine around her hands and feet and dropped her on the ground.

"Let me go! I order you!"

"Shut up, or I'll bind up your mouth as well."

He stood guard in front of her. She shut up, but only so she could hear. The vibrations on the ground grew stronger and stronger and then stopped abruptly. Shi ducked down to see through the mass of legs in front of her. Through the tangle, Shi saw the glint of metal, dark gray metal clad feet. Soldiers, she thought. Ler's soldiers. Then she heard his voice.

"Dryads, I am Leramiun, King of Regia. I am here to offer diplomacy. Like it or not, you are a part of this world. One piece of a whole. You are subjects to the crown. And you have broken laws. Perhaps laws unbeknown to you, but be that as it may, I know you can decipher the difference between right and wrong. And killing innocent people is wrong. I am obligated to bring judgment against you on behalf of the dead."

"We don't recognize your authority!" a warrior's voice rang out.

Oh no. Shi trembled inside.

Everyone lifted their voices in agreement.

Ler shouted over them. "There's no reason to bring this to bloodshed! Our peoples are connected."

"Let me go, Ree," Shi said sternly. "Or, I'll start calling to him. If he sees me tied up like this, he'll advance his forces."

Ree looked down at her, then away. Every soldier took one menacing step forward.

"I want this to be peaceful!" Ler shouted. "Don't force my hand."

The moment teetered on the edge of a knife. Shi held her breath.

"Warriors, stand down!" Fer's voice called out.

Shi exhaled. The crowd parted as Pru came toward her.

"Let her go," he ordered Ree. "We will talk to this king."

Ree's jaw pulled tight, unwinding the vines reluctantly. Pru pulled her to her feet and marched her next to him, his wrinkled hand clasped painfully on her arm. Ler's eyes fell on her, rage flaring in his gaze at the rough way she was pulled along.

"Unhand her," he said through clenched teeth.

Pru shoved Shi at him as though she were a piece of trash. "Thief!" he accused. "You snuck in here and took one of our pure ones like a bandit."

Ler tucked her protectively against him. "Perhaps. But you have stolen more than I. You have taken the lives of more than a hundred. And now blood must be paid. Blood for blood."

Fer turned to the people. "Go back to the Heart while we discuss matters."

The elders came close to Ler.

"Shall I leave you as well?" Shi asked.

"No. You're queen. I need your help with this."

Ler looked back at the line of soldiers and nodded. They stepped back a few paces. Shi looked at them, feeling a sense of dread and awe. There must have been hundreds. The front line, different from the whole, had burnished red metal armor, while the rest had silver. Those in red gave Shi a deep tremble of danger. They carried weapons obviously designed for hacking, flat blades on poles.

"You are the leaders?" Ler asked Pru and Fer.

"We are the elders."

"You gave your warriors orders to kill any passersby, or did they decide that on their own?"

Fer and Pru exchanged a nervous glance.

"There is a great difference between following orders and acting alone. You understand?" Ler said.

"They were following orders, mine explicitly," Fer stated.

"You are taking full responsibility?"

Fer closed his eyes for a second, and then he looked up and lifted his head defiantly. "I take responsibility."

Ler pointed at Pru. "You shall no longer have any authority over your people. And you," he said to Fer, "shall die. The blood will be paid. And your warriors shall be granted clemency. Do you agree with this, Shi?"

Pru and Fer looked at her, their eyes pleading. She wanted to say no. But she couldn't. Ler was being more than merciful. She thought about the dead again and felt maybe he was too merciful.

"I agree," she said quietly.

"Go and tell your people what is to happen," Ler said to the elders. "Say your goodbyes. Execution will be at nightfall."

Pru and Fer turned and walked back. Ler turned to his men and gestured for them to come closer. The front line of red circled close around them.

"Stay here. Make sure nothing happens. Stay on your guard."

"Yes sir," they chanted together.

Ler pulled Shi through the thick of soldiers. They fanned out into the trees around them and after a moment, she couldn't see them anymore. She held herself together by sheer will. Ler looked at her for a second and then removed the armor covering his chest. The second it clanked to the ground, he pulled her hard against him. She buried her face in his shirt and sobbed.

"I'm sorry, Shi. I'm so sorry."

She shook her head but couldn't speak. He anchored her as she cried herself out. Finally, her voice came back.

"Everything's so ugly."

"Yes. It's a bad day. But the outcome is better than I dared hope for. I'm sorry. I didn't mean for that to sound—"

"No. I understand. And you're right. You were so merciful, Ler."

He kissed her. Nothing more than that. Just a kiss that lingered, comforted, and loved.

"I brought you something."

"What?"

"Your crown. I had it made special by my master jeweler this morning."

He pulled a small cloth pouch from a pocket in the side of his boot and placed it in her hands. She undid the drawstrings and pulled the crown out. Shi held it gently, dazzled by its simple beauty. The silvery metal reached up in a perfect imitation of branches, the center set with a pale aquamarine stone that resembled the moon.

"Do you like it?"

Shi snorted. "Silly question."

"It's a tribute to the night we met."

"Put it on me." Shi bowed her head. "How does it look?"

Ler had that same dazed look as the first time he saw her. "Gorgeous."

Shi clung to him, knowing it was a stolen moment and it couldn't last any longer.

"I have to get back and see how everyone is taking the news. They might need me."

Ler kissed her again, swiftly and passionately. "Go," he said. "You're already a good queen."

He watched her go, remembering too late that he was going to tell her about the shadow sand.

CHAPTER 9

Shi walked slowly into the congregation of her people. The elders had already told everyone what was to happen. Pru stopped talking as she approached. All eyes fell on her with many different emotions. Some looked on her with pity, others with interest or trepidation, and a few with anger and accusation. Shi didn't try to cluster in next to the Verdant. She looked pleadingly at Shea. Shea held her face blank for a moment, then everything softened in her eyes, and she reached out to Shi. Shi clung to her for a second then faced everyone solidly. They all noticed her crown.

Pru cleared his throat and continued. "We have feared it may one day come to this. And now the Heart is discovered. I think we might never again have peace."

"It's all her fault!" Ree said, pointing at Shi. A few others murmured their agreement.

Shi stared them down. "How do you know my relationship didn't just save all of your lives?! That Leramiun didn't show you mercy and not take one life for every life taken because of his love for me?"

"That is...probably true," Fer conceded.

"You must all accept that Leramiun will be here often, to be with me. And you should be grateful. He is good and kind. He is not going to harm us, or the Heart. In time, he will come to understand the responsibility of caring for the Heart. I will teach him. The Heart will be better protected than ever before. I promise."

As night kissed the sky, Fer said goodbye to everyone in turn. The mothers took their children away from Fer's tree and tried to lull them to sleep. Everyone else gathered around, sober or crying. The soldiers followed behind Ler. Shi was grateful Ler didn't address everyone again. He looked at Fer and simply asked, "Are you ready?"

Fer nodded and climbed into his trunk. Ler pointed at Fer's trunk and three of the red soldiers came forward and surrounded Fer. They lifted their terrible hacking instruments and began chopping. Four swings each and Fer fell. A cry of sorrow rang out as the Dryads mourned him.

Ler approached Shi. "What should I do now?" he whispered.

"Leave. Let us see to his body. Come back tomorrow."

"Would it be crass for me to kiss you before I leave, given the circumstances?"

Shi smiled sadly. "Yes, I think it might be. Here." She held up her hand.

He took it and placed a kiss on the back of it. Unable to hold her with his arms, he held her with his eyes. Shi touched his cheek.

"Go."

"Until tomorrow then."

Ler left, along with his men, leaving a handful of them to stand guard outside the boundary.

Shi turned, her people were looking at her expectantly. She began singing the song of death. Slowly, one by one, they joined her in singing Fer's requiem. They surrounded him and picked him up, taking him to the Heart. It took the entire night for the flames of the manifestation to consume Fer's body. When he was gone, the Heart sent a surge through the wood, giving back a piece of Fer's life force to everyone. The blessing was bittersweet.

As the dawn broke, everyone, including Shi, climbed into their trunks and slept, exhausted from sorrow and ceremony.

****

Leramiun hardly slept. He lay awake, agonizing over what had happened, questioning if he'd done the right thing, and missing Shi so much it hurt like a fresh wound. He rose early and dressed for the day, unsure how long he should wait to go back to the woods. A special portal would be opened that morning, allowing workers to move in large loads of shadow sand.

In the back of his mind, he thought about the issue of the wizard, and he wondered what had happened to Helena. He looked down at his floor, all traces of blood had been scrubbed away. He decided to try and find her before he did anything else that morning, but as he went to open his door, there was a knock.

Quinn leaned against the doorframe, looking tired and irritable.

"Good morning, brother," he said sardonically. "I've got a problem."

"It better be a good one, because I don't know how much else I can handle right now."

"The wizard, Kracelmunstermier, or some stupid name like that, he says he won't talk to anyone but you now."

Leramiun groaned. "Has he become violent?"

"Yeah, look what he did to me." Quinn pulled his sleeve up, hissing in pain. A perfect handprint was burned black on his forearm. "He said I was insolent, and it just took a second, he laid his hand on my arm then poof, he burned me."

"Damn it, Quinn. *Were* you insolent?"

Quinn scowled and shrugged.

"I need to be with Shi today. We're supposed to start bringing in the sand. Do you think you can oversee that while I sort this mess out?"

"Sure. I'll gladly see to your blushing bride while you're busy. I'll give her kisses for you, shall I?"

"No, but you can give her a letter from me. And stop being an asshole."

Quinn shrugged again and waited while Leramiun quickly scrawled a note, rolled, and sealed it. Quinn put the note inside his vest.

"Remember, you're to act as a foreman. The workers have their orders to keep the sand on the outside. It should come out like a moat. Don't spend much time around the Dryads. They're mourning the death of one of their elders."

"No problem. I assume I'll see you there as soon as you're done placating the refugee. You can't leave Shi alone with me for too long. She may decide she's with the wrong brother."

Leramiun punched Quinn hard in the shoulder. "I told you to stop being an asshole."

"All right, all right." Quinn rubbed his shoulder.

"Is it out of your system now?"

"Yeah."

"Good. Now get out of here. I'll see you later."

Leramiun wiped his mind clean as he entered Fortress castle.

"Your Majesty," an officially dressed vampire greeted him. "So glad you're here. Come with me."

Leramiun followed.

"The wizard's power is brutally strong. So far, he has been very diplomatic and controlled, but Prince Quinn angered him yesterday. We have him in the rune room in an attempt to neutralize his abilities. We don't really know if it is effective or not, so be careful."

Leramiun entered the room. He'd never been in a rune room. The walls were inlaid with stones and symbols. The wizard sat in the far corner, in what looked like a comfortable chair, with a cup of tea on the table next to him. Leramiun could easily feel the power the man held. The air around him rippled. He was dressed in a plain gray cloak, his hair hung long down his back, and he was very tall, even while sitting down.

"Who are you?"

"I am Leramiun."

"Ah yes. The king. I've been waiting to meet you. I am Kracel Murint."

"My apologies. I've had important matters to—"

"Yes, of course. Your younger brother told me about it."

Leramiun scowled at that. "I'm sorry if Quinn offended you. He's young and grieving the recent death of our father."

The wizard looked at him closely and took a sip from his teacup. "I've taken your measure, young king. I am willing to help you. *You* are a good man. You have the makings of a great leader."

"Thank you."

The wizard's eyes became suddenly bright. "Beware of your brother. He is full of malice."

CҺAPTER 10

Quinn bit and drank viciously from Helena before beating her again. He left her unconscious on the floor and headed to the woods. He cracked his knuckles and licked the blood off them, feeling marginally better. Now he was going to go and play with Shi. He knew how to plant himself in a female's brain.

He strolled through the massive open portal into the forest. The work of carting in the sand had already begun. The line of vampires working had already settled into a steady rhythm. They didn't need any direction. That was fine with him. He didn't want to babysit them anyway.

He looked around for signs of the Dryads, but nothing and no one moved at all. He walked in, under the dense branches, where everything became exquisitely beautiful. He walked and walked, trying to find his way back to the waterfall. Finally, he gave up and decided to try something else.

"Shi...oh Shi. Are you here? I've got a message for you."

He turned around and there she was, standing a few feet away. If he just took one step and reached out, he could catch her. He looked her over lazily. The delicate gown she wore clung to her sexy curves, taunting him. Quinn clenched his fists as his anger and desire rose to the surface. They were alone, or alone enough.

Her displeasure at seeing him was carefully veiled, but he detected it nonetheless.

"Why are you here? What is that noise?"

"That noise is the sound of preparation for the little love nest Leramiun plans to build for you and him. Shadow sand from Halussis, placed around this little area to protect against enemies. I'm surprised Leramiun didn't tell you about it."

She regarded him with open irritation. "Why isn't he here?"

Quinn smiled and pulled out his brother's letter.

"Leramiun is busy right now, but he sent you this."

He held it out, but as she reached for it, he snatched it back.

"Just teasing you. Here." He held it out again, but closer to his body this time.

When she reached for it again and he snapped it back, she stumbled forward, right into his trap, and his arms.

"Ah, yes. That's better," he said quietly, pressing himself tightly against her. "Don't I get a kiss for delivering the message?"

He thought she might scream or fight. He hoped she would. It would make everything so much better, but she looked directly into his eyes. It was as if she had jammed her hands into his brain. She saw everything and mirrored the darkness back for him to see clearly.

"You disgust me," she said evenly.

He would have attacked her had she screamed it, but her plain statement of fact removed something from him. She was right. He was disgusting. He shoved her roughly away from him.

"Stay away from me, bitch. If I get you alone again, you're going to be a whole lot more than just disgusted. Understand?"

Quinn turned on his heel and marched back the way he'd come. He'd make her pay. He was in her head all right, not the way he'd wanted to be, but he'd make it count. So he wouldn't ever be her fantasy, he could live with being her nightmare. He made it back to where the workers were and leaned against a tree trunk, staying out of their way. The storm inside him churned. He wanted to go back to the castle and do to Helena what he wished he could do to Shi. He could close his eyes and imagine it was her.

He was just about to do just that when a Dryad climbed out of a tree near him. The man stumbled drunkenly and braced his hand against the trunk he'd just emerged from. Quinn walked over to him. Sweat poured on the man's face and his eyes practically spun in their sockets. Quinn recognized the cause immediately. The Dryad had come in contact with the sand and was deep in hallucination.

Quinn grabbed the man by the arm. "Hey."

The man tried to focus his gaze on Quinn. "What's happening to me?"

"You're reacting to the sand, pretty badly, too, looks like. Tell me, are you in ecstasy or agony? A dream or a nightmare?"

The man began to gasp for breath. "Nightmare...agony," he hissed.

"Good. Very good," Quinn crooned. "Come here, out of sight."

Quinn directed the man away from the line of workers and set him down behind some thick shrubs. The man began convulsing. This was too good to be true.

Quinn rushed over to the workers. "Okay, you are all doing a good job, but you're not putting the sand in the right place. Move it forward into this dense area, as much of it as you can. Put it around the bases of the trees."

"But sire, we were told to keep it to the edges."

"I'm telling you what you need to do now! I'm the prince. Obey!"

"Yes, Majesty."

****

Shi opened the letter with trembling fingers. Her encounter with Quinn had shaken her and made her feel dirty under the surface, where she couldn't wash it away. She exhaled as she read the letter, the words were a balm.

Shi,

I love you. I just realized I haven't really told you that yet.

-Ler

She read the letter a few times. Her exhaustion came back, weighing her down. Shi climbed back into her trunk and fell asleep. She didn't sleep for long. Cries of pain and terror filled the wood. Even before she left her trunk to investigate, a terrible knowledge solidified in her head. Before she even knew what was wrong, the fantasy she had built in her mind, of her future, blew away like leaves in a storm.

Shi climbed out, transfixed in horror. All around her, her people stumbled around, blind, screaming and moaning. Some thrashed on the ground, others lay still...dead. Poison penetrated the ground and floated on the air. Shi ran as fast as she could.

"Shea!"

Hands grasped at her as she ran, bodies on the ground tripped her. "Shea!"

Then Shi saw her. Shea stood against Hul's trunk. Her back arched, her head thrown back, her hands clasped on her belly. Shi ran to her and grabbed her by the shoulders.

"Shea! Shea, look at me!"

Shea's head flopped forward as though her neck was broken, her eyes rolled back sickeningly. Her breathing jolted in and out of her and she began to wail, her hands moving furiously on her belly. *"NOOOOOO!"* she cried.

Shi placed her hands on Shea's belly, and she felt the baby die. The healthy roundness pulled inward like a dried husk. Then Shea fell backward. Shi caught her and lowered her to the ground. Shea opened her eyes and looked at Shi for one moment. Her hand squeezed Shi's arm, then fell limp. Shi screamed in agony and held her sister's dead body against her.

****

The door to the rune room banged open, startling both Leramiun and Kracel. The expression on the face of the person at the door startled Leramiun further.

"Sire, something awful has happened."

Leramiun found himself grasping the arm of the messenger. "What?!"

"The Dryads...they're all dying."

Chapter 11

He ran. He knew he couldn't save her. But he ran. It was happening. Shi was dying, and he couldn't do anything to stop it. He'd never been so afraid. He couldn't think of the pain that would come, only that he must get there in time, and terrified he wouldn't. He must get there in time. He ran. He ran through the portal and hit the ground running. All the workers were gone. Their carts of sand abandoned. He ran into the woods, straight into the choking stillness of death that hung in the air like a haze. Only then did he hear his heart thundering in his ears.

"Shi!" His voice tore through the air. *"Shi!"*

He turned in a circle, bodies all around his feet.

"Ler! I'm here! I'm here!"

He ran again toward her voice, and then he saw her. She was running to him, but she was still a distance away. He ran faster. Her steps faltered. He ran faster. Her arms stretched out to him. He caught her as she fell and went down on his knees. He cradled her head against his chest, and she looked up into his face.

"I held on. I waited for you."

He had so much to say and no time to say it. She was slipping away.

"Shi, don't go..." he whispered. "Don't go."

"Can't... hold...on." Each word struggled out of her. "Got... your... letter..."

She brought her hand up. His hasty, inadequate letter was clasped in her fist.

"Thank...you...Ler. Thank you for your love."

"No, Shi. Thank you for yours."

She drew in a rattling breath, her eyes clearing for a mere second, reaching down into him like a caress. "Goodbye."

It broke him. He couldn't say it back. He couldn't. Goodbye was final. Never would he say it. Her eyes closed. She was gone.

****

A few soldiers found him hours later, lying on the ground, holding on to her body. They tried to rouse him to no avail. They made to lift him, but still he hung on to her. They pulled, using their considerable strength, and still, his hold wouldn't slacken. They had to break his fingers. He didn't respond to the pain. Only after they carried him back through the portal and closed it behind them did he stir. His eyes were blank, but the agony began to rise up out of his lungs.

No one who heard his cries walked away unaffected.

Leramiun appeared mentally catatonic for an entire year. He looked at no one, spoke to no one, his spirit crippled by grief. The workings of the Onyx Castle fell into confusion and then into a lull. Quinn would have taken the throne, had it not been for the staggering evidence against him brought to light by the many workers who followed his orders and became instruments of death to the Dryads.

Kracel Murint took up residence in the castle, on the approval of Leramiun's advisors, moving into a growing position of power, until he had all but taken up stewardship of the throne. No one knew how to stand up to him, and after a while, no one cared to, as he proved to be mild and just.

He imprisoned Quinn, withholding the death penalty, insistent that Leramiun would surface, and it would be his call as to what to do with his murderous younger brother.

Leramiun shuffled the halls like an old man, his eyes open but unseeing. He wandered without destination. Everyone skirted around him. It was the sound of arguing and mocking voices that first jabbed a hole in his opaque mental barricade. Then the sound of a woman weeping, a woman whose voice he recognized, broke him free, and he looked at what was around him.

He was standing in the middle of the harem. Women moved around him as though he were a stone statue, giving him no notice at all. Two women stood over another on the floor, hunched against the wall. They shouted hurtful words at the one cowering, and then one kicked her.

"Give me that ring, hag! I'll tear your hand off to get it if I have to!"

"Stop it!" he yelled, the words croaking out of his unused vocal chords.

The two abusers jumped and looked at him. All the women in the room fanned out, staring at him with wide eyes.

He looked down at the woman on the floor, her face turned to the wall. He knew her. A blue stone ring glinted on her hand. *His ring.*

She looked up at him through tearing, bloodshot eyes. *Helena.* Her gaze hit him in the heart like hammer. She looked broken. Her hair hung in greasy strands, except where it had been pulled out by the fistful. One of her shoulders pulled in wrong as though the bones had been shattered and healed back incorrectly. And her once beautiful face was terribly scarred.

Strength breathed back into him as he strode over and lifted her off the floor. She didn't fight him; she just looked at him in disbelief as he carried her through the castle back to his room. He set her on the bed and left the room. A few minutes later, Leramiun came back with his personal physician.

"Treat her the way you would treat me," Leramiun said to the doctor. "Do everything you can."

The deft hands of the doctor examined her. He spoke quietly with Leramiun before leaving the room.

After that, Leramiun took care of her himself. He drew her a bath, washed and gently combed her hair, and fed her from his own veins. And still neither one of them spoke to each other.

She fell asleep quickly. He tucked her in and sat in the chair next to the bed, watching over her. Every scar on her face convicted him. He would make amends. He swore to himself that night, never again would anyone come to harm because of him. *Never.*

Chapter 12

There was time that was lost. Only an embrace of darkness. But then her spirit awakened. Her consciousness remained. She was dead, but she was still there, and she was alone. None of her kinsmen were there with her. Their souls had flown and hers had stayed. Why? Did she choose to stay? She couldn't remember.

At first, there was just awareness, thoughts. Then came the pain. It began in the feet. Shi looked down where her feet used to be, there was a swirl of what looked like green cloud, twisting upward. It moved up and over her, leaving an oddity behind. She had a new form. Neither woman nor tree, both, merged into one. She had lost all variation of color as well, and was now monochromatic. She didn't think it a pretty green. Not a living vibrant color, but the hue of death. Shi held out her hands and examined them. Her fingers were thin, elongated, and gnarled. Her arms were likewise thin and twiggy. She drifted over the ground, over the dead, and examined the change that had so quickly come over the wood. The whole area was poisoned.

The water now had a purple tinge to the silver. She looked at it, oddly detached, and thankful she wasn't really experiencing her emotions. The Heart called to her. She drifted to it. The manifestation burned high and wide, enveloping the dead trees of the Verdant in dark purple flames. She felt a small flicker of hope that if the flames consumed her tree, she could go to where the other Dryads had gone. But then the flame pulled back and shrank to its usual size. The Verdant had burned to clear. Crystalized.

An unfortunate truth came to her then. She thought she had died steeped in love, and indeed she had, but behind that beautiful tapestry were the other emotions she had died in: rage, hate, and guilt. She was a ghost, stuck forever in the throes of those feelings. She had lost the living's ability to move past something and change.

Years passed. No one set foot in the cursed wood. Shi's existence was solitary. She learned about her limitations and tested what she figured was possible. She found she could set her feet on the ground and walk if she wanted to. She could drift in the top of the canopy but not go past it. With great concentration, she could lift physical objects and hold them momentarily, even things impossibly heavy. After she learned that, she set to work creating a graveyard.

The bodies on the ground turned to piles, like mounds of dried leaves. Shi gathered them and buried them all together. When a tree would fall, she would lift it and take it to the graveyard where it could petrify and become a monument. Shi was impatient for Shea's tree to fall; she had designated a very special place for it.

The day Shea's tree finally fell was marked by another event: her first visitor, and he was most unwelcome.

Shi had just finished moving Shea to her place of honor, when she felt him enter the wood. Quinn.

She watched him from overhead. She was gratified he looked thin and unhealthy at least. He took his time walking around. She could leave him alone if he left after satisfying his untoward curiosity. Shi discovered another unfortunate truth that day. She could hear his thoughts. She could see the fabric of his soul, and it was dark and repulsive. He'd just escaped from prison, and he blamed her for everything that had gone wrong for him.

He found the graveyard. A hateful smile broke over his face as he recognized it for what it was.

"I thought you might still exist," he shouted. "I hoped for it. I have a message for you."

He took a step back, fear plain in his eyes as she came down and materialized in front of him. He tried to cover his cowardly reaction with weak bravado and gave her a contemptuous sneer.

"It is you, isn't it? Yes, I recognize you. Wow, death was unkind. You're hideous."

His mind revealed things she had wondered about for years, ever since she died. He was the real murderer of her people. The introduction of the sand was Ler's stupid mistake that Quinn used as a weapon.

"Why are you here?" It was the first time Shi had spoken since she died, and her voice sounded foreign to her own hearing.

His mind answered her question before his mouth could. Killing her hadn't been enough for him. Now he was free from prison, he'd come to hurt her again. The images in his head staggered her. Images of Ler.

"I came to tell you that he never really loved you. He has mated again, and they are expecting their first child. The whole kingdom eagerly awaits the birth."

Flashes of images in Quinn's mind seemed to confirm his words. Shi looked impassive, but internally she was raging.

"You ruined everything for me, Shi. Your death should have broken my brother beyond repair, the fact that it didn't is further proof he didn't love you. Sure, he moped around for a while, but then, just as it was time for me to take the throne, he snapped out of it and became *the best king Regia has ever seen.*" He said the last bit in a singsong. Clearly quoting what others were saying about Ler.

The rage was building.

"And you, you were so easily replaced... Why won't you speak?" His rage at getting no response almost matched her own. He shrugged and touched one of her monuments. "I guess you must not have loved him either. Too bad, you obviously loved your own kind. Too bad you killed them all for a man you didn't even love."

Shi's scream shot out from her like a shockwave. The energy ripped through everything around her, breaking the monuments she'd lovingly created. Quinn was thrown backward against her sister's tree, his bones shattering throughout his whole body. She moved and bent over him, his heart thundering in her ears.

"Look at me," she ordered.

He did, his eyes the only parts of his body that still worked.

"All these years, your desires to use me as a rag went unfulfilled. Now, I'm the one who's going to penetrate you."

Shi reached her hand through his chest and grabbed his heart. She held it tight, constricting her fist tighter and tighter until her fingers punctured the fleshy outer membrane, deeper and deeper until it stopped beating, the aberrant organ skewered on her hand.

Shi wept as she surveyed the damage to the graveyard. She couldn't fix it. She tore Quinn's body to small pieces, scattering them evenly on the ground in the center of the graveyard. She offered the guilty blood to the ground where she had laid the dead to rest. The offering wasn't enough, but it was something.

Shi left the graveyard and abandoned her efforts there. She buried herself in her old trunk. For decades she slept. Time meant nothing. Sometimes she would awaken suddenly, a sense of someone just beyond the boundary. Whenever this happened, it was accompanied by the faint sounds of weeping. Ler would come to the edge, but he never crossed into her space. Then he would be gone again, before she could move toward him.

She stayed numb. She went back to sleep. Time meant nothing.

****

Tentative steps woke her. The woman's thoughts whispered through the woods to Shi, as quiet and gentle as the rustling of her skirt along the ground. Shi jolted as she realized who the vampire woman was: Ler's queen. Shi's knee-jerk ire faded away as soon as she examined the woman's intentions and character. She wasn't there looking for Shi. She was curious about the place and the terrible incident she'd heard about for so many years, and she wondered about the Dryad woman who had captured Leramiun's heart.

Shi came closer, keeping herself invisible, surprised at the woman's appearance. Under the many scars on her face and neck were the traces of her lost beauty. Shi dug into the woman's mind for her name. Helena. She carried many scars on her heart as well. But she also had joy. A terrible, jealous ache spread through Shi as she looked at images of Ler and Helena's children.

Helena spoke, not realizing anyone could hear her. "This changed him so much... Such a terrible thing." Then she hissed angrily, "Quinn."

Shi watched Helena's memories of Quinn and what he'd done to her. And how Ler had rescued her, restored her, and had given her the throne regardless of what anyone said.

"Hello," Shi said quietly.

Helena jumped and looked around. Shi remained invisible.

"It's you, isn't it? You're her? You're Shi?"

Shi didn't answer.

"Forgive my intrusion. I meant no harm."

"Don't fear. I won't hurt you...not like I did Quinn."

Helena gasped. "Quinn? Quinn came here?"

"A long time ago. I killed him."

"Good. I'm glad to know for sure he's dead. There were no reports or sightings of him after he escaped prison. His crimes convicted him to death, but after all that happened, Leramiun couldn't bring himself to end anymore life."

Shi's memories came rushing back, along with the rage. It flooded her, pushing out reasonable thought.

"You should go," Shi warned. "I'm volatile and I might change my mind about hurting you, unjust as it might be. I'm not sure I can control myself."

Helena didn't need telling twice. She moved swiftly out of the wood and was gone. Shi trembled against her emotions, trying to ease them back. The images she saw of their children, children with Ler's eyes, gave her a strange crushing feeling, and yet she was glad they existed.

As the years wore on, more people came to the wood, some by accident, some seeking it out. Shi talked to none of them. She would riffle through their minds for lack of anything else to do, but she left them alone. Mostly, she slept, cocooned in her old trunk.

When Ler finally came, he came at night, and he came alone. She felt him like a hook through her core. She drifted, invisible, over him, amazed at the time that had passed. He was an old man. She looked inside him and saw the disease. He was dying.

"I've come back, Shi," he whispered, moving slowly toward the falls.

He squinted, his sight failing, as tears ran down his aged cheeks. He reached the beach and fell to his hands and knees, his shoulders shaking as he cried. His pulse labored, weakening. She caught him as he fell forward and turned him over to look up at her.

"Shi...there you are, my love."

Her hands clenched tightly on him. "Why are you here?" She flashed back and forth internally from love to hate, unable to make it be still.

"I came here to die. You died in my arms, now I can die in yours."

"Beg! Beg my forgiveness! I'll never give it. Beg anyway."

"No," he rasped. "No, I won't. The fault lies with both of us... I wish I had died next to you. You were my only love, Shi."

"And what was Helena?" Shi demanded.

"Obligation. Hate me if you must, but you can't stop me from dying where you are. Since you left, it's all I've wanted...just to die where you are."

He was right on the edge. Death slipped up behind her and reached its hand out for him. Racked with sobs, swamped with too many conflicted feelings, Shi acted without thinking. As his spirit lifted from his body, she seized a hold of it and shoved him backward.

"No!" she screeched. "You can't move on while I'm stuck here forever alone."

His spirit looked just as he had the day she mixed her blood with his, right there on that beach. Death came back around and reached for him again. Ler began to fade.

"No!" she screamed again, gasping at him. She caught his arm and pulled him to the Heart. "I curse you to torment, Leramiun! I bind you here with me forever!"

She grabbed him by the shoulders and shoved him into her trunk. She turned around and faced down death. *"Mine!"* she shouted at the hovering shadow.

Death hesitated, then backed away. "For now," he whispered.

CHAPTER 13

"Forest, Forest wake up." Shi shook her shoulder gently.

Forest came to groggily, her head throbbing painfully. She sat up, her eyes clearing. Shi's face came into focus next to her. Forest felt like she'd been beaten up as the effects of the sand wore off. Her heart ached with the knowledge she'd just acquired.

"I understand why you didn't tell me."

"You should go home now. It's late."

"He's still here, isn't he?" Forest asked.

"Yes," Shi whispered, looking down.

"Wow. And you still haven't forgiven him? You've kept him caged all this time?"

"Time doesn't matter that much to the dead, Forest," Shi hedged.

Forest looked at her severely for a moment before shrugging. "Whatever. Keep living your lies. I've butted in to your business enough for one day."

Forest got to her feet and dusted off her butt. She turned her ring around in her hand, but before she could go home, Shi reached for her hand.

"I love you, Forest."

"I know. I love you, too."

"Love Syrus better. Love him more. Appreciate every moment. Tragedy can happen to anyone at any time."

Forest nodded "You're right, Shi. I'll do that. Do you want me to give you some space for a while?"

"No, daughter. Visit me when you want to."

Forest hugged Shi gently, opened a portal, and went home to Syrus.

****

The night came in, soft and warm. Shi felt emotionally bludgeoned after having to watch everything Forest saw. She had never experienced their history like that before. She drifted to the flame. The thorn of rage that had been stuck in her ghostly heart for so long dislodged. She laid her hands on her trunk. She felt him from deep within lay his hands against hers. Just a faint vibration of energy from him tested the barrier.

Shi sighed and moved the breeze past them. It whispered a promise of coming absolution as it danced through the trees.

The End

Acknowledgments

I have to give a big shout out to my editors: Amanda Fiske, Jen Duffey, Ally Robertson, and Brynna Curry. Thank you so much for your invaluable help! A huge dose of love for my writers group. My undying gratitude and love to my wonderful family. But most of all, a big thank you to YOU! My readers are the best! Your love and support keeps me plunking away at the keyboard, and lifts me out of my emotional valleys. Thank you!

Sneek Peek of THE LEGENDS OF REGIA- DARK SOUL
The third full-length book in Tenaya Jayne's spellbinding series.

COMING SOON!

Prologue

Regia, fifty years ago…

Years of combat in the royal army, stringent training for the Crimson Brotherhood, and seven medals celebrating Mycale's honor and bravery amounted to nothing with two katana in his back. The flames consuming his house lit up the night as the acrid smoke of burning wood and flesh filled his lungs. The screams of his life mate and children caused his body to jolt, adrenaline attempting to force his body to accomplish the impossible. As he struggled to get up, the blades were thrust deeper, pinning him to the ground.

Mycale had never failed in anything, ever. But now, he'd failed to protect that which he loved the most. His family died thirty feet in front of him while he lay powerless to save them. The screams of his son and daughter quieted and he knew they were dead, but one moment before Geanna's life was extinguished her voice cried out to him.

"Mycale! I love you!"

And then she was gone, before he could answer and tell her for the last time that he loved her. The spiritual bond of destined life mates crashed within him, utterly demolished the second she died. The light inside his heart turned black, the atriums and ventricles broke apart. He wanted to crawl into the flames and die beside them, where he belonged.

The blades impaling him slid back, removed from his torso. The rush of blood from his wounds soaked the ground beneath him. He attempted to pull himself forward to the house when a foot kicked him over on his back. The light of the fire moved along the length of the sword now pointing at his heart. Mycale looked up into the eyes of his best friend, Steven. And his broken heart broke a little more.

"Why?" Mycale rasped, his lungs full of smoke and blood.

The lifeless expression on Steven's face flinched, smoothed out again, and then crumpled completely.

"I'm so sorry. I'm just following orders," Steven's voice broke and he looked up at the burning house, tears running through the soot on his face. "The wolves will be blamed for this and the entire peace treaty will be forgotten."

"Geanna…the children…How could you?"

Steven closed his eyes and shook his head. "I'm sorry."

Steven stood directly over him, the hilt of his sword clasped in both hands, lifted over Mycale and plunged into his chest.

****

The deaths of Mycale and his family was the catalyst to end the fragile diplomacy that had been formed between the werewolves and vampires. And it worked, the treaty died. Mycale, however, did not. The sword through the chest missed his heart by a breath. Hours later, lying half-dead next to the pile of ash that used to be his home, Mycale was tripped over by a werewolf on the run.

Tek clambered to his feet, cursing whatever obstacle had tripped him and was immediately shocked from his thoughts of running as he surveyed the macabre scene in front of him. He crouched down beside the body at his feet and felt for a pulse. The light thump of the vein beneath his finger had

Tek cursing again. Taking a deep breath, he grabbed the vampire by the arm and hefted him over his shoulder.

Tek labored under the dead weight. The constant flow of obscenities running through his head was directed at his mother's memory for teaching him to always help those in need, friend, stranger, or foe alike.

The pale sun broke the horizon and seemed to taunt Tek. He wheezed under his new burden, a nasty cramp in his leg and a shooting pain under one shoulder. He couldn't continue on in broad daylight with a charred heap of vampire across his shoulders, despite the fact he was traveling off the road.

Tek looked around. He had no idea where he was. The distant sounds of civilization made him apprehensive and hungry at the same time. Unloading the man on his back to the ground, Tek began scouting a place to hold up for the day.

An hour later Tek was cursing his mother's memory again as he dragged the unconscious vampire into the obliging cave he'd discovered. Propping him against the moist rock wall, Tek did something he'd never done or even thought about before: he placed his forearm against the lips of a vampire. Still unconscious, the vampire opened his mouth and bit down.

Three gulps and the vampire's crusted, bloodshot eyes sprang open, latching on to Tek's like a vise. He watched as the vampire threw himself back, clutching and beating at his chest.

"NO!!" his cry of agony resounded off the walls.

Tek grabbed the young man by the forearms and had his seized in return. The vampire's eyes locking onto his again. Tek was no stranger to suffering, his own and that of others, but these eyes burned with the torture of the damned to a level Tek had never seen.

"You saved my life?" he demanded.

"Yeah, I did…And I can tell, you're not about to thank me for it."

Tek let go and tried to back up. The devil in those eyes wanted his blood, and not just for a light snack.

The vampire grabbed at his sides but found only empty sheaths, his weapons gone. His eyes shot back to Tek. "I'd appreciate it if you'd kill me now."

Tek blinked. "Aren't you polite."

"Just lend me a weapon, I'll do it myself."

"I'm sorry. Unfortunately, I'm completely unarmed."

The vampire got to his feet, brushing past Tek as he looked out from the entrance of the cave.

"Where are we?"

"No idea," Tek answered. "I left my last dwelling with the thought *anywhere but here.*"

The vampire turned. "Why did you save my life?"

Tek shrugged. "Morality. It's a serious flaw...You're a royal soldier?" he just noticed the embossed emblem on the scorched, damaged breastplate.

The vampire blinked confusedly for a second before looking down at his chest. His hands touching the holes through the metal. The next second he was ripping the armor from his body. Tek backed away from him as he caught the look in his eyes. How could eyes go dead and still burn like that?

He watched from the mouth of the cave, as the burned soldier limped off a ways and began to bury his armor in the ground under a tree. He saved only a ragged scrap and used its sharp edge to carve into the tree trunk. Tek turned away from the sight, as the vampire's grief began to pour out of him. He knew, unquestioningly that crossing his path, into the middle of this terrible crime and the pain resulting from it, would change Tek's already complicated life. He just couldn't yet see how.

Tek came back to the cave's opening at the sound of uneven footfalls.

"I wasn't sure you'd come back."

"Neither was I," the soldier conceded, turning the rough scrap of metal over and over in his hand. "I must disappear...I must bide my time..."

Tek smiled ruefully. "Me too."

"I won't thank you for saving my life. As far as I'm concerned, I died last night with my family...But my body is still animated for one purpose... revenge."

Tek ran his hands through his hair and sighed. "I don't know where I'm going, or when I'll stop, but you're welcome to come with me, provided that you don't slow me down."

The vampire turned his dark eyes to the ground, one hand rubbing a spot on his back. "I didn't heal completely, and after this amount of time, it means I never will. I'll probably always limp, but I'm still strong and well trained. I could watch your back."

"Okay," Tek extended his hand. The vampire caught it firmly and held fast. "My name's Tek. What's yours?"

Hesitation filled the vampire's face.

"I'll use any name you give me," Tek prompted. "Pick a new one."

The vampire nodded, hesitating again. "Merick. Call me Merick."

Chapter One

Unseen. That was how she lived, not one single soul had laid eyes on her in over a year. Solitary, she kept to the wilds and retreated whenever anyone wandered too close. She talked to no one except herself and sadly found her own company distasteful. High on a great precipice, she looked out over the world and could see all the way to the rose-colored Crystalline Sea, the setting sunlight glinting off its jagged waves. She sighed deeply at the approaching, desolate night. Lonely and bored to the point of unqualified despair, Netriet ran her fingertip along the sharp edge of the rock she'd found earlier. Its flinty weight felt rough and dirty in her palm. She contemplated the edge and what she could do with it.

Will you please stop trying to kill yourself?

"I would if you'd go away."

We both know I can't do that.

"I promise not to try to kill myself for the rest of today if you shut up and not say another word."

The shadow was silent for one minute before she began to hum a disjointed tune in the back of Netriet's mind. Netriet took a deep breath, trying not to give in to the tears of defeat layering under her eyelids. If only it could just be over, but the shadow never let her harm herself. When she focused on benign or pleasant things, the shadow would be quiet and retreat to the corners. But before long, before Netriet could really relax and breathe peacefully, the shadow's sharp fingers would start to scratch and pick at her tendency for negativity, prod deeply at her fear, and tickle the longing for revenge.

Sometimes she fought it. Sometimes she won. But when her defenses were down, the shadow would wrap its arms around her and whisper in her ear, skillfully seducing her into submission. Netriet hated her own weakness. The blackness of her scars and the dark tendril that circled her left eye bespoke of the disease within. She ached to get back at the persons responsible for all of her trouble...The elf woman who first put the collar on her hand and sent her to Philippe. She was the catalyst. And the transparent being in the Wolf's Wood who prevented her from dying and placed the shadow within her. Netriet didn't even know their names, but their faces were forever branded in her mind.

You want revenge, don't you?

"Shut up."

Why do you keep us out here away from everyone else? You'll never get your revenge like this.

"I'll never get revenge regardless."

Netriet looked down on the rising smoke of civilization as the closest town built their evening fires. A sharp-toothed wind picked up around her, sliding through her threadbare clothes, biting at her skin. She huddled down against a large tree trunk, wrapping her arm across her knees. How long could she go on like this? She often desired food but since her transformation, no longer needed it to survive. She existed with no purpose and no prospects, an entirely pointless entity.

Let's go back. The shadow crooned in its most seductive tone. *You're so lonely. I know you'd like to see your friends again. Huh? Forest? The ogre lady, Martia? She said she wanted you to come back. You never did. That was rude of you.*

Netriet sighed and shook her head. "I can't. I won't let you hurt anyone."

I wouldn't! I promise. Why do you think I'm so bad? I save your life almost every day.

Netriet ground her teeth. "You don't care about me. You're just afraid if I die, so will you."

Not true. I care about you. That's why I want you to go back. You've been through so much. I want you to have some happiness. Otherwise, why would I tell you to go see Forest? I hate Forest. But I'll suffer her company because you like her.

When Netriet made no more reply, the shadow fell silent for a while. Sleepiness came upon her.

You're cold...So, so cold...wouldn't you like to have your shawl back? The one you lost? You know where you lost it. We could go find it. You wouldn't have to see anyone if you didn't want to...Remember how beautiful it was? Remember how sweetly it smelled?

Weary, frustrated tears slid down her dirty cheeks.

Admit it. You want it back.

"Of course I want it back," Netriet hissed. "I admit it. Happy now?"

The shadow said nothing. Netriet waited. Nothing. Damn it. The shadow had baited her successfully. The memory of the patchwork shawl twisted through her like the pain of a loved one's death. And with the image dancing in her mind, she felt a ravenous desire to hold it again. The shadow was right; she did know where she'd lost it. If luck was with her, she could find it in the moonlight and be back to the safety of seclusion before the next morning's sun reached its pinnacle.

Netriet stood up and headed off into the darkening shadows of the thick wilderness. She walked at a steady pace, ever vigilant and aware of her surroundings so as not to be caught off guard by a stranger. The darkness bothered Netriet, but the shadow reveled in it, guiding her through effortlessly. The faces of people she cared for shimmered in her mind. Netriet abruptly dug in her heels.

"No. I've changed my mind. I'm going back."

Are not.

The shadow moved under her skin like oil and shoved her forward from within. Netriet stumbled as her feet picked themselves up and down against her will.

Look around you. You've never gone that far away from where you really want to be.

The shadow was right. She hadn't moved far past the fair, or from Forest's land. She'd wandered in vast looping circles, but the fair and the hope of acceptance there had remained the unacknowledged axis of her world. She marched on, unnaturally strong, her body never tired. The sight from her dark eye sliced through the night easily. As she came close to the outskirts of Forest's land, a headache began vibrating deep in her skull and she unconsciously started backtracking. She shook herself as her marvelous sight made out the edges of an invisible barrier, like a huge dome of energy. She reached out her hand and walked forward, experimenting. She couldn't touch it. There was nothing tangible to touch but the magic there held her off like a magnet pushing away.

Netriet's face was caught between a smile and a grimace. There was no way she could cross onto Forest's land now. What had happened to cause

Forest to need so much security? She continued walking along the edge of the protected barrier coming close to where she'd been chased by two werewolves, where she lost her shawl. Her memories of that night came back into sharp focus. Any signs of the struggle were long gone. She walked along, her eyes searching for the brightly colored fabric and abruptly everything in the terrain changed from the way she'd remembered it, so much so that she questioned if she had somehow lost her way.

The Fair had moved, not away but out, expanding. What she saw in the distance hardly resembled her memories. The evidence of construction was everywhere. Trees cut and cleared, a partial wall in the early stages of erection circled the extended parameter, and little houses replaced many of the colored tents. The ragtag camp was becoming a town.

Netriet approached quietly, continuing to keep an eye out for her shawl, but her attention was caught on what the people of the Fair had done, wishing she knew the answer as to why? The area of the wall obviously designated as the entrance propped up a dozing werewolf, fudging his guard duty. She laughed internally. Anyone taller than a child could easily get over the under-construction wall. In fact…that was exactly how she intended to get in.

****

Forest hunched over the lengthy report on her desk and pinched her tired, stingy eyes shut for a moment. She knew you couldn't throw centuries-old traditions of a world in the fire without there being some hang ups. The knowledge however hadn't stopped her from wishing. She pushed back from the desk, suddenly aware she was totally alone. Forest swore, realizing she'd lost track of time and would be home late, *again*. If she didn't get home in the next few minutes Syrus would start to worry. Forest rolled the papers up and tucked them under her arm before closing up her office. Kindel and Ena must have gone home for the night hours ago. As soon as the door was locked, the magic protecting it pulled together over the door.

Forest yawned as she strode out into the foyer, the heels of her boots clacking loudly on the stone floor. She turned the ring she'd made from her

End of the Bridge, around her finger so the silvery ball rested in her palm about to send herself home.

"Goodni…" her farewell to the security ogres trailed off as she noticed there were none.

Forest's sleepiness vanished instantly as she turned around, her hand on the hilt of her sword. She was alone, or seemingly.

"Hello?" she waited a beat. "Security?"

Adrenaline poured into her stomach as a whispered laugh echoed around the room. Forest drew her sword as a figure stepped out from behind a column across the room. The young woman wore a green hooded cape and an expression of amused insolence on her pixie-like face.

"Madam Hailemarris, I presume?" she thrust her hands out with a flourish as she gave a theatrical bow to Forest.

"Who wants to know?" Forest demanded.

The young woman tisked. "We've been watching you. You're quite the crusader, aren't you? A real idealist trying to make a difference."

"I assume I've stepped on your toes in some way. Put a family member of yours away? And you're here for revenge, or you want a favor and have brought a bribe?"

"Oh no. No bribe. As I said, we've been watching you. And apparently, you can't be bought."

Forest curled her lip at the young woman. "That's right. So what do you want?"

The young woman sighed and pulled a crossbow from her cloak, training the sight on Forest. Forest eyed the weapon for a second before sneering contemptuously.

"Apparently, you haven't been watching me for very long if you think that toy in your hands can subdue me."

"Not scared?"

"Not in the least."

The girl shrugged and dropped the crossbow. "I guess I wasn't the right choice as messenger."

"Deliver your damn message and be done with it. I want my dinner."

The girl brought her foot down on the crossbow. The arrow shot across the room towards Forest's feet. She moved to the side but the arrow pulled a line behind it like a harpoon and the tip was hooked not pointed. The cord hit Forest's ankle, the end swung around, and dug into the leather of her boot before retracting backward, pulling Forest off her feet.

She managed not to crack her head on the floor, coming down hard on her elbow instead. Forest cut the cord with her sword and scrambled to her feet, her eyes darting around. The girl had vanished. Laughter echoing around the room again.

"Now that I've taken your ego down a notch, maybe you'll give me a little more respect."

The girl strode back out from the shadows.

"Clearly you're here for games, but I'm in no mood to play."

The girl laughed, her voice changing into a deep baritone as she shifted into a tall werewolf. Shock and disbelief filled Forest. She'd never seen or heard of a shifter that could shift into the opposite sex.

"You'll play if I say so," it said.

"Who are you?"

A twisted smile broke over the big ugly face. "I like how you're using your manners now. I am Shreve, captain of the Aluka circle."

Rage began a controlled boil in Forest's head. "The insurgents."

"I don't care for that term, myself. We prefer to be called-"

"I don't give a damn what you want to be called. I'm placing you under arrest."

"Really? You and who else?"

Forest advanced on the shifter. It slunk to the side and began to circle, shifting again into a beast form, it's arms elongating and mouth stretching over pointed teeth as a snout protruded.

"You can't win," it slurred, the beast's mouth now shaped only for tearing flesh not talking.

"I'm a shifter too. Just because you look like a werewolf doesn't mean you're strong like one."

Shreve lifted a heavy arm into the air and brought his fist down on the floor, the stone breaking under the force of the blow. Forest lifted one eyebrow, trying to conceal her surprise.

"Okay, so you're a freak. But then you must know, so am I."

Forest threw her sword down and disappeared using her elfish ability. Shreve's eyes darted around as he moved forward. His nostrils flared in an attempt to sniff her out. Forest moved behind him, grabbing a stone bust of late king Leramiun off its stand and throwing it like a football into the back of Shreve's head. He stumbled and went down onto one knee. Forest ran up his back, digging her heels into his flesh as she went and launched herself off his shoulders back towards her sword. She rolled as she hit the floor, grabbing her sword. She faced him, dropping her invisibility, as he got to his feet.

Forest charged Shreve head on, slashing a deep gash across the chest and spinning quickly away as it swung its huge arm at her. It roared, slashing at her with its long talons ripping through the back of her shirt. Forest jumped over a sweeping strike meant to knock her feet out from under her and sliced another line on the side of Shreve's neck. He sank back to one knee, trying to hold back the blood gushing from his wounds.

Forest brandished her bloodied blade at Shreve, who cowered backward. "You're under arrest."

Shreve's hand shot out, the talons shifting into long elf fingers as they grasped Forest's wrist. Shreve stood upright now in the form of a male elf with the signature red eyes of the *Rune-dy*, pushing down on the pulse in her wrist as his wounds mended before Forest's eyes. She stood face to face with him, her arms going limp, as his eyes drilled into hers, scattering her thoughts, making her sleepy. He took her sword easily from her hand.

"Look at you, so easily hypnotized. Maybe Copernicus was wrong about your power. No matter, you're the leverage we need."

He hooked the blade under the chain of her Hailemarris necklace. The light flashed off the metal into Forest's eyes breaking his mental grasp on her. She blinked, twisting her ring back into her palm and thought of home as she grabbed at her sword trying to take it with her as the End of the Bridge pulled her through the black portal to safety. Forest landed on her hands and knees in her garden, without her sword, and a slice on her hand.

Syrus instantly grasped her shoulders and picked her up, holding her against his chest. "What just happened? I was making dinner and I got the terrible sensation you were in danger. I was about to go to your office. Are you alright?"

Forest clung to him, shaken to her core. "No. I'm not. I was just attacked in the foyer of Fortress by a… I don't know what."

Syrus hooked his arm under her knees, carried her into the house, and set her down on the couch. "Now, tell me."

"It was one of the insurgents, said its name was Shreve."

"*It?*"

"Yeah. I've never seen anything like it. At first, it was female then it shifted into a male. And when he shifted into a beast he had the strength of a beast. I got the upper hand, about to arrest him, then he shifted into an elf and he… mesmerized me, or something." Forest looked at her bleeding palm. "Shit. He got my sword. Hold on, I've got to call Redge."

Forest pulled her phone from her pocket and dialed Redge.

"What can I do for you, Forest?" he answered.

"I need you to get your team and go to Fortress. I was just attacked by one of the insurgents. They took out security. I had to use my portal to save my own neck I wasn't able to check on them. I'm sure the insurgent is gone by now, but get any evidence you can. And be careful. I don't know exactly what we're up against here."

"Understood," he said sternly. "I'll report back as soon as it's done."

"Thanks Redge."

Forest put her phone down on the coffee table and sighed. "Well, that was embarrassing."

"What was?" Syrus asked, looking at her palm.

"I just got my ass handed to me."

"I'm sure you got some licks in."

"A few, but..." Forest hissed in pain as Syrus shot a few red sparks from his fingertip into her wound, sealing it instantly. "You're really good at healing now."

"The new masters give me plenty of practice when they hack on each other during sparring," he chuckled, pressing a kiss onto the place he just healed.

Forest exhaled her stress. No matter what was happening, so long as she had Syrus, she was okay. Forest placed her hand on his cheek and looked into his grey eyes. She loved him more every passing day. He was her home, the stronghold for her heart.

"So, you made a new formidable friend, who took your sword, did you learn anything else?"

"Yeah, he dropped the name Copernicus, and said I was the leverage they needed."

Syrus went very still, the color draining from his face.

"What?" Forest asked.

"Damn it," he whispered, gathering her into his arms.

"What is it?"

"You don't know the name Copernicus?" he asked.

"It sort of rings a bell, but I don't know how."

"Let's hope, for all of our sakes, that the one now calling himself Copernicus, is an imposter."

****